MORE FUTURES

A Charity Anthology

FOR FERALS

Edited by:

Danielle Ackley-McPhail

eBooks

Pennsville, NJ

PUBLISHED BY
eSpec Books LLC
Danielle McPhail, Publisher
PO Box 242,
Pennsville, New Jersey 08070
www.especbooks.com

ISBN: 978-1-965266-21-2
ISBN (eBook): 978-1-965266-20-5

The docked ear cat logo is the logo of A Future For Ferals Cat Rescue

Copyediting: Greg Schauer
Cover Art and Design: Mike McPhail, McP Digital Graphics
Interior Design: Danielle McPhail

Licensed via www.shutterstock.com
Banner: Silhouette of vector black cat © artsara
Break: heart shapes within the paw pad © Md Abdus Sahid

 OUR COOL CATS

Marc L. Abbott	Eric Hardenbrook
Danielle Ackley-McPhail	Kris Katzen
Rigel Ailur	Anton Kukal
Charles Barouch	Sharon Lee
James W. Bates	Will McDermott
Grace Bridges	F.R. Michaels
Christopher J. Burke	Nancy Jane Moore
Amber Davis	Lisanne Norman
Jacob Jones-Goldstein	Patrick Thomas
Brad Jurn	Sherri Cook Woosley

Global Cat Day and National Feral Cat Day
October 16
https://globalcatday.org/about/

While there are many, many rescues across the country and around the world, here are a few we've come across that we wanted to share.

Alley Cat Allies
https://www.alleycat.org/ -

Humane Rescue Alliance
https://www.humanerescuealliance.org/

eSpec's interns, Shiloh and Karma, thank you for your support!

FOR OUR ANGEL CATS
ALWAYS IN OUR HEARTS

Bandit (Mau)	Ralph	Pepper
Tiger	Marguerite	Ariel
Bootsie	Chauvelin	Mimi
Hootch	Percy	Frankie Blue-Eyes
Mandy	Marie	Ash
Kat	Duchess	Burton
Baby	Nikki	Archie
Alley	Rigel	Arwen
Goodyear	King of the Jungle	Brandee
Rex	Lister	Buzzee
Kismet	Joby	The Rev
Cuddle Bug	Nelly	Nicky
Merry	Tal	Patia
Curio	Bast	Kodi
Magnus	Bonnie	Max!
Tuppence	Clyde	Hex
Echo	Duzell	Socks
Munchkin	Molly	Mozart
Mithril	Rascal	Scrabble
Audrey Kitty	Trooper	Belle
Benjamin	'Neaker	Sprite
Daisy	Miss Audrey	Trooper
Nevar	Benjamin Franklin Cat	Quill
Bleys	Hobbs	Peppercorn Underfoot
Mahasamatman	Boodles	

AND FOR OUR "COLONY KITTIES"
YOUR PERSON LOVES YOU EXTRA-SPECIAL

Spot (Sweetie)	Eve	Squeaks
Spec	Midnight	Jean
Karma	Gizmo	Storm
Shiloh	Tigger	Roguee
Pandora	Logan	Boris

eSpec's assistant office manager, Spec, endorses this message
and thanks you for your attention.

PLEASE, PLEASE READ...

I'M NOT USUALLY BIG ON INTRODUCTIONS; HECK, A LOT OF PEOPLE DON'T even read them anyway, but here it goes. In all of my years of compiling anthologies it has always been about a cool, fun idea. A concept hits me, a catchy title follows along and I am off and running!

This one isn't any different in that regard, except it is.

A Future for Ferals has a heart, and a cause. (And a sequel!) The title itself is taken from the name of a cat rescue run by a former coworker. In our time together on the clock it was difficult not to get caught up in the real-life drama that is cat rescue. I heard all of the stories, from late-night trapping sessions to being called in to clear out a cat hoarder's house to whatever other adventure came next.

Rescue is not an easy calling, whether it is cats or some other species. It is hard work with usually no pay, often not enough volunteers, and very little thanks beyond (hopefully) the satisfaction of making life better for another living creature. When donations are low, rescuers draw on their own funds to take care of their temporary charges, and not even just the basics of food, shelter, and necessities, but medical costs or even end-of-life care.

This collection seeks to share some of that burden. The profits from the campaign that funded these books have already been sent to A Future for Ferals, a 501c3 registered charity, to mitigate the costs of rescuing over fifty cats in one day from a hoarder house. Of the fifty cats, only two had been neutered. The vet bill was over $4000 to neuter the rest and take care of the necessary medical care some of the cats needed resulting from neglect.

This is one group of many around the world seeking to make life better for abandoned and feral cats (and other animals) and the communities where they live. We and our authors would like to support them in their efforts.

All of the stories you will read here have been donated. All of the profits from future sales will be donated to various cat rescues for the lifetime of this anthology.

Given the nature of the book, some of these stories are reprints, others are newly written. And for once, the genres are mixed, so my apologies in advance if not all of the stories are to your taste or the collection feels uneven. In the interest of not getting monotonous, they aren't necessarily all about cat rescue, though all are about cats. What we have also done, however, is include personal accounts between the stories, as well as short informational pieces about various aspects that go into cat rescue. Why? Because cat overpopulation is rapidly increasing and any effort we can make to educate and improve that situation helps.

We hope you will enjoy everything we have brought together, and share word of this collection with others. Perhaps even gift a copy to someone you know has a heart for the kitties as well.

Thank you for reading…

Danielle Ackley-McPhail
Editor and Publisher

Our office manager, Spot, aka Sweetie. She keeps us in line, though productivity is not always her goal.

A FUTURE FOR FERALS
CAT RESCUE

A FUTURE FOR FERALS CAT RESCUE IS A 501C3 NON-PROFIT FOSTER-BASED organization that was started in 2021 to specifically help the cats that are typically overlooked in a normal shelter setting when it comes to adoptions such as older cats, disabled cats, those with behavior issues, and more. We got started after our founder worked in a county shelter and saw the total disregard and lack of care when it came to these types of cats there and knew something better could be done for them.

A feral cat is an unsocialized cat that does not want to interact and will typically avoid humans, with that being said "a future for ferals" means to us less euthanasia of feral cats especially in the county shelters, more socializing when and if possible, more barn homes when absolutely needed, more trap, neuter, and return (TNR) and definitely more public education and compassion for the topic.

Other than adoptions, our other heavily focused goal is TNR and spay/neuter in general to help reduce the cat population. The world is currently in a cat overpopulation crisis with there being more cats than homes for them available. We will never adopt our way out of the population crisis without TNR/spay and neuter of all cats. Since starting the rescue in 2021 we have been able to help TNR hundreds of cats each year and that does not even include our adoptable cats being spayed/neutered, or our outreach program that we offer to assist our local communities with low cost spay/neuter appointments. We believe every cat should be spayed/neutered as both genders becoming territorial and acting out if hormones are not in check. Avoiding these things happening will in turn help with less surrenders and less abandonment, which is why we offer an outreach program for low-cost appointments.

We are completely foster-based, meaning we have volunteers who open up their homes to our cats and take care of them until they are adopted into their forever homes. We do not have a physical location with an adoption center like a typical shelter. This unfortunately does limit us with intakes though, as we can only intake if we have a foster home lined up for that cat. We often have over one hundred cats in foster care awaiting their forever homes, with many being long-term residents due to the types of cats we focus on, but since starting in 2021 we have successfully adopted out over five hundred cats into loving homes. We would never have been able to do this without having such wonderful fosterers offering assistance.

Angelina Commisso

A Future for Ferals rescue

CONTENTS

Rex

STRANGELY FAMILIAR
Sherri Cook Woosley

APPLAUSE ERUPTED FROM THE STANDS WHERE THE UPPERCLASSMEN watched the plebes compete for their next mission. Seven teams of battle mages paired with feline familiars hoping for a placement where they'd be in direct action against the Necromancers from the north. It was a constant war each spring as the death mages sucked the energy from the living to power their armies until they retreated before icy winter. Even now citizens crowded the main road of Queen's Capital to take refuge behind the city's protective gates.

In the arena of the Queen's Military Academy, Sandy's tail flicked back and forth, giving away her anxiety. It was hard for her to get a read on the other six cats, even though they were supposed to be on the same team. Many familiars and their humans developed a shorthand for communication; some partners could even establish telepathy, but the other cats seemed to have their own feline communication that excluded Sandy. The other cats were all black, muscled, and formidable. Most were from bloodlines of other familiars. Exactly what one would expect in a companion to a battle mage. Sure, there were differences between the cats. Betta was slender and could stretch farther than the others. Duke had white on his chin and paws and was the most friendly. Thad was built thick and could jump on and off a moving broomstick with ease. And then there was Sandy... a gangly, scraggly cat with nondescript fur the color of dirt.

"This is the last event. As long as we don't move down the leader board then we'll still have the fourth pick." Betta dropped her chin to pin Sandy with her stare. "Don't mess it up."

Thad coughed in a feline version of a laugh.

Embarrassed, Sandy shifted her shoulders. This one spot between her shoulder blades had been itchy for days. She jutted her head forward and used her hind leg to scratch. As she did, a patch of fur flew off and floated to the ground. Frozen, with hind leg still extended, Sandy looked at the other familiars, hoping no one had noticed. They were all staring at her.

"Ewww," Betta said, finally. "Your fur just fell off."

"The orphan has mange." Thad flicked an ear. He would do anything for Betta's approval. "That's how she's going to fight the Necromancers. Poor Jaxon."

Orphan. It was true. She had no idea of her parents or her breeding or where she was from. Sandy's whiskers drooped. The other cats could make fun of her, but she hated it when they brought Jax into it. He was everything a young mage should be: talented, smart, ambitious, and kind. Only she knew he wasn't as confident as he appeared, that he practiced and studied for hours to mask his fears of letting the team down.

Commander Michaels, the officer in charge of this class of mages and familiars, announced, "Our last exercise will be a speed and agility course on broomsticks. It will be slightly different than in other years." He stood unmoving in his crisp uniform as whispers swept through the teams. "Necromancers have recently employed skeletal birds in their strategies to take out our battle mages while they are casting spells. Familiars will need to protect our mages while they are vulnerable. To simulate the situation, upperclassmen on brooms will be flying at the riders."

The audience in the stands whooped and stamped their feet in delight at the new challenge while the teams pulled together in a huddle to discuss strategy.

Jaxon strode toward Sandy wearing his ceremonial black robe over trousers and carrying his broomstick. A thrill of pride swept through her when he gave her a wink. She wasn't sure what humans considered handsome, but she liked that his eyes softened when he looked at her, when he slammed his spellbook shut to signal studying was over, when he'd talk to her as he moved throughout the dorm room, his voice a gentle wave, rising and falling depending on the subject.

Now Jaxon set the broom in a horizontal floating position like the other riders. Cooper, Betta's mage, pointed toward the third hoop. "That's a set-up for an attack because you'll have to line up to fly through. Watch for it." He held out a fist and Jax tapped it with his own. "Ride on, brother."

Betta's tail twitched as she narrowed her eyes at Sandy. Sandy did not need telepathy to understand the message.

Settling into position on the broom, Jax signaled to Sandy.

She leapt onto the back. Jax's broom rebounded, and he grinned back at her. "Big breakfast this morning?"

Embarrassed, Sandy flattened her ears. Yes, she'd been eating more lately; it was like her stomach couldn't stay full.

Then the starting bell rang and brooms soared into the air. This was Sandy's favorite part as the wind pressed her whiskers to her face and sounds grew distant. Flying equaled freedom.

Two other brooms pulled ahead but Jaxon leaned forward to close the gap. Then another broom passed them. Was she slowing Jaxon down because of her weight compared to the other familiars?

His broom glided over the first hedge and he maneuvered low to clear the next obstacle of branches. Sandy ducked but their broom was shoved to the side as another rider came through at the same time. Sharp stick ends poked Sandy in the side as Jaxon struggled to free the broom. He wedged his boot against the trunk and kicked off. Their broom shot forward and approached the rider who'd smashed into them.

Neck and neck they raced toward the third obstacle. Sandy looked up and saw an upperclassmen woman in a red cloak sitting on a broom, waiting. Her black feline licked her lips. Sandy meowed in warning and Jaxon pulled to the side, peeling away from the hoop. They would have to double back, but it was worth it. The woman plummeted down in a move the plebes hadn't learned yet. With a shove that looked nonchalant, she slapped a glowing bubble on the rider that meant they were out.

"I'll bring us around and cast a spell as we approach," Jax shouted back to Sandy. "Can you keep me covered?"

Sandy meowed an affirmative into the wind.

"We're one of the slower teams but as long as we don't get out then we'll still finish ahead of everyone with a bubble."

Sandy nodded, even though he couldn't see her. Jaxon had brought them back underneath the branches of the second obstacle. He set the broomstick toward the hoop and began chanting. The woman in the red cape, meanwhile, turned her head back and forth as she searched for them.

Their broom streaked forward toward the hoop. Sandy pushed back into her hindquarters so that she'd be able to bat at the woman. The upperclassman locked onto them, her broom tip pointing as she aimed for the spot where they'd emerge from the hoop. There was no way to avoid her. Sandy lunged forward and her claws snagged on the red cloak even as the woman slapped a bubble on Jaxon's shoulder.

They flew to the end of the course and stood with the rest of their team as they moved down the leaderboard to dead last. Sandy's heart dropped, too. This was her fault. She'd slowed them down by being too large and then hadn't been able to protect her mage.

"We'll get them next time," Jaxon said to the team and then turned to repeat it to Sandy.

That is so like Jax, Sandy thought. *Always sensitive to everyone else even though he is disappointed in himself.*

The crowd in the stands swept down to congratulate the winning teams. Captains took the envelopes with their mission. Riders, including their team, went off to have a drink before packing up to leave in the morning. So only Jaxon and Sandy were still in the arena when Commander Michaels approached with their team's envelope.

Jaxon ripped it open. His eyes scanned as he read it while Sandy scanned his face, looking for his reaction.

"I understand, sir." Jax looked up. "This pass would allow Necromancers to march straight toward Queen's Capital, but they haven't attempted it in generations. Why not?"

"Unclear." Commander Michaels cleared his throat. "Our spies have reported that the locals say there are creatures in the mountains around the pass. Until the past year or so, they've been guardians and did the job for us."

"But not anymore." Jax frowned.

"If they ever existed."

Jax tapped his index finger against his lips. Sandy recognized it as his thinking pose.

"There's something else." Commander Michaels shifted his weight. Whatever he was about to say made him uncomfortable. "You were slow today and clumsy. In battle, you need to watch the troops below so you can protect them. To do that, you are vulnerable. That's why we have familiars. I don't think Sandy–"

Sandy's body turned cold. She wanted to curl up and hide her face.

"Sir." Jax's tone was respectful but cold. "A familiar is a personal choice. I trust Sandy with my life."

"I hope you're right. Because Necromancers won't just put a bubble on your back." Commander Michaels pivoted on his heel and marched out of the arena.

"Come on, Sandy. It's been a long day." Jax gave her a distracted smile, and they set off for the dorm on Jax's broom.

Home was a dorm that the academy provided. Battle mages had their own suite—a necessary accommodation when living with a familiar. The kitchen was small but adequate, with a bedroom and bathroom for the human and another room for them to set up for their familiar. Jax had a soft sofa pushed against the window so Sandy could sleep in the patch of sunlight throughout the day. Then he'd moved his desk into the room, stacked his favorite esoteric tomes along the wall, and engineered a basket onto the end with a cushion inside for Sandy. That way, she could be near him, comfortable, but he wasn't giving up any of his precious workspace.

As soon as they were in the dorm, Jax went to this desk and pulled out two different books. "I want to get a better idea of where we're going tomorrow and what the commander meant about guardians for that pass."

Sandy leapt into her basket and settled, her gaze intent on Jax's furrowed brows. His lips moved as he rifled through the pages. Sandy felt calm and safe watching him as if she were fulfilling a sacred duty. She'd never asked the other familiars if they felt like that—it was too personal.

Sandy's tail twitched. If he wasn't sleeping or getting some dinner, he should at least be looking over spells. Wanting to be a good familiar, Sandy did what Betta would. She leaned forward and swatted the pages to mess up Jax's place.

"Careful!" He gave her an irritated glance as he paged back. "This is a special edition. That's not like you."

Sandy sank back into her basket. She couldn't do anything right.

"Awww," Jax said, expression softening. "I didn't mean to snap. I guess you're right, and I should study spells instead of chasing folklore." He reached out to rub behind her ears. It was her favorite spot, and she leaned forward. Then he scratched down her neck to the itchy spot between her shoulders. Sandy tried to pull away—remembering too late the way tufts of fur had fallen off earlier—but Jax stood up to better examine her back. "Uh oh. Looks like you need some medicine right here. It's rubbed raw."

Her shoulders relaxed. That was the thing about her human. He didn't judge or think she was strange; instead, he loved her the way she was.

As he daubed on a stinky ointment, Jax said, "Our team—mages and familiars--needs to trust each other starting tomorrow. I know everyone is mad about the assignment because we won't see any combat." He shrugged. "My parents aren't from Queen's Capital. In fact, I'm the first battle mage in the family." He chuckled. "I was supposed to work in my father's blacksmith shop, but I couldn't stand it. He thought he could shape me like he shapes hot iron, but that's not how it works with people. Or cats."

Sandy purred in encouragement. Jax had never shared this before, and she didn't want him to stop.

"He burned an entire stack of my books one time. Made me stand there and watch the pages blacken and then curl into the flames while the bitter smell filled the air…" he shook his head. "It was the worst moment in my life. But I didn't give up on who I was. When Commander Michaels came through the village to recruit, I signed up. And now I'm surrounded by more books than that version of me could ever have imagined."

Jax wiped his hands on a cloth and then gestured to the books pressed cover to cover on his desk. "I'm never going to lead our squadron. That's Cooper. I'm not charismatic or charming like Julian or even quick-thinking like Lila. But I'm a hell of a researcher who masters spells that require finesse." He tapped his chest. "Knowing myself means I don't have to compare myself to the other mages. Make sense?"

He waited for her to purr. "I chose you, Sandy. And you chose me, right? No matter what." He leaned his forehead down, and she pushed her forehead against his, and they exhaled, her breath mingling with his. They'd done it ever since she was a kitten.

"Now," Jax said, shutting the book, "you wanna get some sardines and call it a night?"

"I don't suppose I should be surprised that Sandy brought us to a giant litterbox." Betta clawed at the dun-colored ground at the vee of the pass. Tall, craggy sides of the mountain extended to the east and west while they'd come up from the south and set up tents here, the most level spot they'd found. It was best, Cooper had said, to pretend there was the slightest chance that Necromancers would attempt to cross here.

"Where is Sandy?" Betta made a point of looking all around even though Sandy was sitting right in front. "She's in her natural habitat."

"I didn't mean to mess up," Sandy whispered. "That was a new exercise."

"Oh, well, you can explain that to the Necromancers when they attack Jaxon. Just tell them that you weren't ready."

The image of Jaxon bleeding filled her head leaving Sandy speechless.

"Oh, Dirtball. Did your human step on you this morning? No wonder you wanted to be invisible," Thad joined in. "What happened? Did Little Orphan break her tail?"

"You do seem to have a talent for finding new ways to be gross." Betta twitched her whiskers.

Sandy bared her teeth at the other cat, but that didn't stop the other familiars from staring at her tail. If she'd had Jax's delicate skin, her face would burn red.

During the night, she'd had dreams about the pass they would defend. She saw the rocky crags and caught sight of the magic users on the other side. Magic users who used forbidden blood magic to mimic death. Some looked more human than others, but all had the same red eyes. In her sleep, she'd fought—kicking her back feet and swiping her claws. Her tail had flicked back and forth. She'd assumed the pain was from hitting something with the tail's tip–but when she cleaned herself, she'd been startled to see that the end of her tail seemed to have broken. Unfortunately, it now resembled a triangular tip. Or, as Betta suggested, like someone had stepped on and flattened the end.

"Maybe it will give the Necromancers a good laugh." Betta put her nose in the air and fluffed her perfect black fur.

Duke stepped forward as if to intervene, but Sandy turned away and wrapped her tail around her legs, hiding the deformed tip.

"This is our first mission, we must take it seriously. The ground troops have been here for several weeks. They are camped on the side of the mountain between any attack and our mages. Being higher means that our mages can ride brooms out over the troops. We are even more important. Our humans can't see, smell, or move like us," Duke said. "They are like newborn kittens."

"Except they don't even have any hair."

The familiars coughed at Thad's joke.

Duke paced in front of the others. "Remember what you learned when you accepted your true name. That's where our power resides." He tilted his head to hear better. "They're coming."

Yas wrapped her tail around her legs more tightly; Betta licked her flawless fur but watched the tent from the corner of her eye as the mages emerged from their meeting.

Sandy only had a minute to decide. Jax needed a familiar who would help during military maneuvers and keep him safe. Instead, he'd chosen her, and she wasn't good enough. She was heavy and her tail was broken, and she couldn't stop eating. But if she disappeared, Jaxon wouldn't be allowed to fly in battle because he wouldn't have a familiar. For Jaxon, she bounded away, up through boulders toward the peak of the mountain.

It was almost like there was a path because her feet knew just how to climb the boulders and push off to the next one. Once, pulling herself up beside a thin tree, her paw smacked down into the dun-colored dust and there, fossilized by the right mix of heat and rain, a larger paw print already existed.

Thunder rumbled and Sandy lifted her nose to the breeze. She'd never been here before, yet it was all strangely familiar. She continued climbing as the sun set until she reached the entrance to a cave. Inside, the temperature was cool and refreshing. Her eyes could easily see in the low light and she approached the lake to drink the clean water. Drawings covered the cave walls and Sandy recognized the red eyes of Necromancers and saw cat-like creatures with wings attacking them, biting out the red eyes.

The storm arrived with a dramatic downpour of rain, echoing through the mountains in a way that Sandy hadn't heard in Queen's Capital. For once, despite the climb, she wasn't hungry. Sandy stretched out on the cool rock of the cave and closed her eyes, her body relaxing as the image of Jaxon's bleeding body floated away. It was, in a way, similar to the ceremony to find her true name. That's what all the familiars did. They fasted and then stayed in a dark room until they "found themselves," whatever that meant. The problem was that she'd panicked in the dark all by herself. Memories had stirred, fears had welled up, and she'd bolted from the room. True names were secret, so everyone assumed she'd completed the ritual.

In truth, Sandy remembered little before Jax found her… and had no desire to revisit those few memories of strange sounds and smells, feeling trapped and helpless. She shuddered. It was better to remember the moment in the street near the market. Like tonight, it had been raining; big drops splashed into her fur and matted it down. The smells of meat cooking on grills had enticed her from the shadows, but humans were everywhere. She'd dodged heavy boots stomping this way and that in overwhelming chaos, only to have a tremendous muddy puddle splashed on her by a passing cart. Hungry, scared, and soaking wet, she'd lifted her face to the storm and opened her mouth in a piteous meow. Suddenly, two hands were around her, lifting her from the mud, and she was staring into warm brown eyes. Within moments, Jax had pulled off his outer shirt and wrapped her in the clean cloth. Then he'd gone to the nearby stall and purchased a skewer of meat and vegetables. As Jax carried her back to his dorm, they'd split the food, a square of grilled pepper for Jax and warm meat for Sandy, until she fell asleep, happy with her full belly. He'd officially declared Sandy his familiar the next day. Somewhere between sleep and wakefulness, she could still hear Jaxon shouting her name.

Sandy's eyes popped open and she scrambled to the front of the cave. Yes, that was Jax's voice, calling for her through the storm. She plunged down the path toward his voice, agile in the mountains, and her heart almost broke when she saw her beloved human completely soaked, dark hair plastered to his face, hands bloody from grabbing at rocks.

"Sandy," he called, voice hoarse but the relief clear.

It was easy and right to get beside Jax and herd him into the dryness of the cave. Inside he shrugged off his backpack and took out the waterproof bag to start a fire. There weren't very many sticks this high, but it was enough for him to lay out his shirt to dry and warm his hands.

Later, when he'd stopped shaking, Jaxon used one of the branches to explore the paintings on the cave walls.

"Sandy," he exclaimed, squinting in the torchlight. "You're so clever. These are the guardians from the folklore. These are pictographs of lamasu!"

Sandy herded him back to the fire and curled up around Jax so that her body heat would warm him as the fire died out.

Soon the rain stopped and brilliant stars lit the clear sky. Sandy sighed with contentment. It had been wrong to leave Jax. They belonged to each other and now she understood that.

Sandy led Jaxon down the path toward the tents. "You are definitely taller, Sandy. You're twice the size of Betta. No wonder you've been so hungry. We're going to have to get a bigger broom."

She looked over her shoulder to give him a look just as the screaming started. They rushed down, rocks rolling out underfoot, and past the tents to join their team.

"Necromancers," Cooper said, unnecessarily.

Their battle mages rode skeleton elephants among their troops, and their general was inhumanly large, riding the skeleton of a creature with six legs and a horned skull. Most fearsome, two necro-birds, large enough for saddle and bridle, clung to the side of the mountain, their Necromancers small specks of red on their backs. The birds had intact beaks and talons, but all the flesh had rotted from their ivory bones. Necro-birds were fast and precise––nightmares for human battle mages on broomsticks.

Sandy's muscles bunched, ready to attack. The skeletons had unearthly red eyes that glowed in an eerie similarity to their Necromancer. She wanted to claw their eyes out and shake the bones to destroy the corrupt power that held them together.

"We have to let Commander Michaels know," Jax said. "No one has any idea they're here. If we don't stop them… we need reinforcements on the way, and I'm the only one who can cast the communication spell."

Sandy heard what he didn't say: if the Necromancers won, then they would advance across the mountains with their tainted power, killing every living thing and manipulating bones and blood for their own consumption.

"Stay here and cast that spell." Cooper mounted his broom. "For the rest, let's ride. For Queen's Capital!" He flew out over the ground troops.

In response, the necro-bird on the right shrieked an ear-splitting call to battle. The Necromancer army charged up the hill toward the pass.

Cooper waved the ground troops forward from the back of the broom. Julian leapt onto his broom and soared into the sky to take a position at the front of the battle mages. The necro-bird on the left launched higher and then plummeted with talons extended toward Julian. Thad's fur raised across his back, ready to protect Julian. Julian yanked on the broom and threw his weight to the side so the skeleton missed.

Dave's battle mage, skilled with crystals, held up her staff. Orange current sizzled toward the necro-bird, and the Necromancer pulled the reins, banking to the left, on the defensive now.

Jax pointed the broom toward an overhang and Sandy jumped on.

Suddenly, a shrill scream split the air overhead; the other necro-bird had arrived. Like the first, it had attained height and now folded its wings with extended talons. They were trapped. Jax's mouth hung open as he stared upward. Sandy could tell he was running through scenarios, but she already knew there was no way out. Jax's job was to protect his country and the troops below.

Her only job was to protect Jax.

This single thought brought clarity. Nothing else mattered. This was the bond that she and Jax had made to each other when they became familiar and mage. Calm, outside noises muffled, Sandy measured the distance between the closing bird, the floating broom, and the overhang. She and the other familiars had been trained to go for the red jewels that animated the skeletons: break the eye and say goodbye. The Necromancer would feel the recoil and be vulnerable for several moments after.

Close enough to feel the wind from the necro-bird's wings, Sandy leapt upward. Her hind feet pushed against the broom, thrusting it toward the overhang to safety for Jax's spell. The bird instinctively grabbed Sandy and pulled into the sky to avoid hitting the rock walls. Below, she heard the crash of the broom breaking against rock and hoped that Jax had jumped off.

Inside the skeletal claws, Sandy fought against the ivory bones. Her mind and heart were in sync. This was who she was: Jax's guardian. There was a sound like ripping cloth and a flash of pain down her back. Magic tingled, more sensation than pain. Her first thought was that the necromancer was doing something—sucking her life force out. But the buzzing sounded inside, spreading along her spine, shoulders, and haunches. Sandy's joints popped. She felt, somehow, larger and stronger — more herself. And suddenly, Sandy filled the bird's grip, her transforming body pushing against the corrupted bones so they couldn't quite close.

Twisting, she reached her right paw through the talons, delicate as she'd been with Jax's bestiary, and pulled herself up toward the chest. She wasn't trying to escape; instead, she climbed the skeleton toward the necro-bird's head. It was easier than she'd thought — her weight dragged the bird down. Its wings beat harder, and the Necromancer on its back struggled to see what was happening. His face was pale; his skin stretched tight, and his mouth and nostrils were black holes. His eyes, however, were a brilliant red.

They showed a flash of fear as he saw Sandy.

"A guardian!" He turned his head to yell toward his army, "The guardians ARE here."

Sandy's tail, the triangular part, whipped against the belly of the bird, and cracks appeared in the bones. Confidence growing, Sandy growled a challenge, but it wasn't a cat's meow. Instead, a roar echoed off the rock walls.

Realizing the danger, the Necromancer stabbed Sandy with his staff, jabbing through the bird's bones. With a feline grin, Sandy raked her claws against the leather flight straps holding the Necromancer onto the saddle. While he struggled, she finished climbing. It was almost too easy. With her body hugging the skeleton like a ladder, Sandy scratched her paw around the right eye socket. White dust fell, the jewel popping out and shattering on the rocks below.

Frustrated, the Necromancer urged the bird to shoot up higher into the sky. Maybe he thought she would be scared? Sandy bared her teeth in fierce joy. Not anymore. Cold wind whipped past as they went higher and higher. Looking down, she saw the battlefield. Their troops had suffered losses, but so had the Necromancers. The gap was secure. By now, Jax should have been able to call in for reinforcements. Sandy imagined the other familiars watching, wondering what she was doing crawling inside a bird skeleton, but the thought brought no shame. She was who she was meant to be.

With a curse, the Necromancer jabbed Sandy hard in the ribs, knocking the breath out of her. She took quick, shallow breaths as she scratched her claws against the other eye socket, blinking the dust away that caught in her own eyes. This side was harder; she didn't have the right angle, and the Necromancer had wedged his leg into the bird's ribcage to stay on. She felt the sting of metal as he cut her flank, but she gave one more scratch, imagining it was the Necromancer she was gouging.

The red jewel fell through the air.

Sandy and the Necromancer watched, his mouth open in a scream, hers closed with acceptance. When the magic jewel shattered into red dust, the bird's skeleton turned to dust. Sandy and the Necromancer plummeted through the air.

Instinct prompted Sandy and she didn't question it. No more denial. Sandy lifted her chest and arched her spine. Wings exploded from her back. The Necromancer's body dashed against the outcrop at the top of the trail, but Sandy's wings lifted her so she had time to see his broken body turn to dust. And then she glided down past the gap and lowered to the spot where Jax's broken broom pointed toward the overhang. She rushed forward when her feet hit the ground, but she couldn't fit under the overhang. She dropped to her belly and had to crawl inside.

Jax leaned against the wall, shaking, his hand across his abdomen. When he looked up, his eyes widened with fear. She smelled his blood. He'd been hurt.

"Lamasu," he whispered, trying to press back into the rock. "The guardians."

Determined, Sandy pushed herself closer. It was complicated to maneuver the wings, and she huffed as she pulled in one and then the other, like she was working an unfamiliar muscle. She had to 'find' each muscle first.

Her hind feet were flat behind her so she could get her shoulders inside. Betta would die of laughter right now. Again, the thought brought nothing but a sense of understanding of who Betta was.

Jax closed his eyes and began muttering. Was he trying to cast a spell?

Confused, Sandy pushed forward until her forehead touched his. They exhaled together.

Jax's eyes popped open. "Sandy?" His voice shook.

She tilted her head, and his shoulders relaxed.

"You're amazing." He let out a helpless laugh. "I'm looking at myths in my books, and you were right in front of me. Is that what you were trying to tell me? It that why you took me to the cave?"

It wasn't, but she was feline enough not to admit it.

They both crawled out from underneath the overhang. Sandy shook off the dust and then nosed at his robe. Understanding her demand, Jax pulled aside his black robe to show his wound. It looked painful but not life-threatening. Still, he needed to get to a med mage.

Overhead, a fresh team of battle mages flew by. Commander Michael's reinforcements. That meant the troops would be here soon. Lightning sparked beyond the gap, and three booms resonated.

Sandy waited patiently as Jax leaned against the rock to stand up straight. Something was different, though. She'd always looked up to him from the ground, and now they were eye-to-eye.

He shook his head and reached into his pocket. "Necromancers couldn't get through because this gap used to be protected by Lamasu. But you're the missing piece." He unfolded a picture torn from the bestiary. The image was a beautiful, tawny creature like a lion with feathered wings. Gold hoops hung from her ears and encircled her front legs. Her shiny claws were an inch long. "I believe you were stolen from here to be sold on the black market. That's why the other Lamasu won't guard the pass anymore. They aren't here because they are looking for you." Tears filled his eyes. "This is your home."

She huffed. Silly human. Then she nosed the broken piece of his broom.

"Yeah." Jax ran his hand through his hair. "I'll have to get a ride back with—"

Now, she rolled her eyes. *You are mine, and I am yours.*

Sandy lowered herself next to Jax. The silly human finally understood. He threw a leg across her withers—as clumsy as the first time she'd tried to hop onto a broom—and she ran forward and spread her wings. Unlike the broom, where she'd always been an uncomfortable passenger, now they really were free. They flew higher and higher in a widening gyre as Jax laughed and hung on to her neck. She couldn't wait to stare down her nose at Betta and the other familiars. Then she and Jaxon would have to find the other Lamasu. They'd have to figure out what it meant when a familiar was as big as a lion—and had wings. They'd have to… but that was all for another day.

"Oh, man," Jax leaned forward to shout over the wind, "How am I going to feed you now?"

THE RIGHT WAY
Lisanne Norman

ALIA, ON THE EARTH COLONY PLANET KEISS, WAS A VIBRANT HUMAN spaceport town where along the main street indoor markets vied with each other to offer the inducements of all-day breakfasts and other "super-tasty" meals. "English breakfast with cucumber!" signs glowed from every quarter, interspersed with those for "Sholan Pastries, fresh today!" "Chemerian beer!" "Keissian brandy! Nothing stronger!" Spicy tidbits on sticks like kebobs, many sold by street vendors, were everywhere.

Jane strode purposefully along the street, ignoring the stalls, brushing an impetuous Jalnian out of her way as he thrust a skewered lizard in her face, his rapid-fire common port lingo lauding its unprecedented taste and freshness.

Behind her, three of her crewmembers hurried to keep up as they wound their way through the food aisle.

"Why cucumber?" asked Alan, one of the other two humans present. "It doesn't exactly go with eggs, sausages, and beans."

"No idea, but I could use a pastry," Steve said, glancing hungrily at the stall laden with pastries and other sweet confections. "I didn't have time for breakfast before Jane hauled us out here."

"What're we doing here anyway?" Alan asked, adjusting his ball cap as he continued to eye the bounty surrounding him. "No one told me, just said come."

"Going to Joe's Spares," said Harran, their feline Sholan crew member, flicking his tail. "The nav system had a hiccup as we came in to the 'port and we need to replace the wiring. Comes from running the Trader on a shoestring, parts get worn out before being replaced."

"It's easy for you to talk," said Steve. "You Sholans have big budgets for ships."

"Hey, I'm not from one of the big merchant families. We gotta make do too," Harran huffed.

"Cut it out you two," said Jane slowing down as they left the food court and entered the grimy area where repairs and spare parts could be had. The smell of oil and grease fought with the scents of the food in an unpleasant mélange. "It wasn't penny pinching this time, it was the rodents infesting the lower cargo level and ducts. Right, Harran?"

Harran sneezed, his sensitive nose complaining at the smells. He angled his ears toward Jane. "Yeah, they chewed up the LADAR installation really well."

"Any idea which of these traders we're going to?" asked Alan.

"We're going to Joe's trading booth. If no luck, we'll have to search what the others have on display and ask them," she said tersely. "Bloody rodents. Captain said to find a solution for them, he wants them gone now. They've cost us in partial cargo losses and repairs. How we're going to get rid of them I don't know. Traps and poison didn't work." She swerved in her tracks and headed for the nearest booth.

The stall was like all the others. Arranged on the counter were an assortment of the more common small parts that needed frequent replacing. Beside them sat a catalog reader to look up the larger pieces available in the back, or that could be ordered—for a price.

"Greetings, I'm Joe," the owner said, peeling himself off the side wall where he'd been slouching as they approached. "What can I get for you today?" He put his coffee mug down among the greasy rags covering one corner of his counter.

"We need a wiring loom for a GMX Tivo 6500 series LADAR rig," said Jane.

"Not often those go wrong," he said, pulling the reader round to face him.

"Rodents," she replied tersely. "Must have gotten on at one of our stops."

"Yeah, they get everywhere now," said the man, punching his keyboard and checking the screen for results. "Getting to be a real problem. And not just mice and rats, but other species from Jalna and the Chemerian worlds."

"We've suffered enough losses from them, this is the last straw," said Jane.

Harran was picking idly through the goods on the counter, checking out the boxed items.

"Careful there," said Joe, glancing over at him. "They're new in today. Won't fit your ship. A standard Chemerian rental I bet, though one of the better ones from the LADAR you want."

"No," said Alan. "It's a Sholan cast off, still serviceable but getting on."

"Sholan, eh?" said Joe, glancing up at Alan then at Harran. "Guess your captain made himself a friend then, unless he is Sholan?"

"No, I'm the only Sholan on the crew," said Harran.

"Got something here that'll do," Joe said, turning his attention back to Jane. "One is a new unit… the other is reconditioned." He turned the screen to face her. "Reconditioned one is quite a bit cheaper. Comes with the usual recon warranty. Doesn't cover getting munched though," he laughed.

Jane frowned, tossing her dark plait back over her shoulder as she looked at the screen.

"Harran," she said, gesturing to him. "Check it out. Nav's your baby."

Harran moved forward to check the specs on both units and groaned inwardly at the price of the new one.

The owner added, "The recon one is in back here. It's from a good source; I've done business with them before. A new one will take a week to order."

"The recon one looks okay from the specs," said Harran, tapping the screen with a claw tip. "I'd need to see it. Steve, you better come too since you'll be installing it."

"Be my guest," Joe said, lifting up a portion of the counter and ushering the two of them in.

They followed him into the back shop where rows of shelving held neatly stacked and labelled parts. Joe led them over to a shelf where several multicolored wiring looms lay stretched out.

Harran and Steve picked up the connections, checking them out, seeing that the joints and wiring were all intact. "That'll do," Harran said. "Can you have it delivered to bay C3 later today?"

The owner looked at the communicator on his wrist. "*Hmmm…* Can do, but it will be late afternoon. That all right?"

"Yes. That will give me time to remove the old one before it arrives," Steve said, following Harran as he pushed his way through the aisles of shelves back to the counter.

"All settled," Harran said to Jane. "It'll do us fine. He'll send it over this afternoon."

"You'll be paying for it now, I assume," said Joe, shutting his counter up again.

"Yes," said Jane, handing over the ship's account card.

As he was processing it, Joe looked up. "You know if you want to get rid of that rodent problem, you can't do better than get yourself a cat or three. There's plenty running wild around here. They're natural predators for small things like mice and rats. They're clean and look after themselves. Just clear out their litter box, feed and water them, and they'll be happy as sandboys."

"It's a thought," Steve said, looking over at a burly cat weaving its way down through the people toward the food court. "Unless, Harran...?"

Harran hissed, lowering his ears briefly in annoyance. "Don't even think it."

"Just joking," said Steve hurriedly.

"How do we get hold of these cats?" asked Jane as she finished their transaction.

Joe shrugged. "Catch 'em. They belong to nobody out here. Those folk with pet ones keep them mainly indoors because of the local wildlife. Food's always a good incentive to these ferals."

"What kind of food?" asked Alan.

"How should I know?" said Joe. "I sell ship parts not solve rodent problems! Something like they'd eat in the wild, maybe, not spicy, though. You got the whole food aisle to choose from."

"That Jalnian and his lizard kebobs would do," said Harran, remembering the annoying peddler.

As they began to move off, Joe called out, "You'll have better luck finding them in the back alley than the main street!"

"I can't believe we're even considering this," said Jane, shaking her head.

"Dibs on not doing clean-up duty," said Alan, settling his baseball cap more securely on his fair hair as a gust of wind came down the walkway, threatening to blow it away.

Back to the food area they went, Harran buying a couple of the roasted lizard tidbits from the hawker.

Steve pointed, indicating a gap between two stalls just ahead of them. "There's a way into the back alley there."

They headed toward the opening as Harran gingerly held the meat offering, trying not to let it drip onto his hands.

The back alley was a dumping ground for all sorts of rubbish, primarily food-prep waste where they were, as well as older and smellier offerings. There were a couple of cats nearby, and looking down the alley, they could see more scrounging round the piles of leavings surrounding the large, overflowing dumpsters.

"Don't they ever empty their garbage?" muttered Alan.

"Just a thought," said Steve, "but what're we going to carry any cats we capture in? I don't fancy just holding them. Likely they'll squirm to get free, and we'll get shredded."

"Good point," said Jane. "I'll head back to the main drag and see if I can find anyone selling bags. There should be ones big and strong enough to prevent getting clawed."

She was back in five minutes with a heavy kit bag. Meanwhile, Steve had been trying to lure one starveling cat toward a portion of the food, while the other two had been looking out for other likely candidates nearby.

"Not that one," said Jane, shaking her head. "It might be diseased. It's too thin for what we want. Aim for the healthier looking ones."

"If any are healthy in this environment," muttered Harran, dividing up the meat into small chunks on the paper tray he'd been given with the kebobs.

Steve stood up and turned toward the others who were eyeing a small tabby cat playing with a piece of paper waste nearby.

"That one," agreed Jane as Steve tried to approach the cat slowly.

"Here puss, puss," he said softly, holding out the morsel of food. The cat stopped playing and stared at those intruding on its domain. As Steve bent down and moved slowly forward, hand held out, it skittered to the side, avoiding him.

"Throw it the meat." said Harran. "We can make a trail of it leading to us if it takes that piece."

Steve threw it toward the tabby. It landed short but it did get its attention. It stretched out its neck, sniffing the air before looking at the group of three people.

"There's too many of us," said Harran. "The rest of us need to move further away."

"If you're so knowledgeable about this, why don't you do it?" Steve asked quietly as Harran handed him the plate of meat then backed off.

"Cats don't usually like me. They see me as a bigger predator than them," he said as Jane and Alan joined him a few feet away from Steve.

"Uh huh," said Steve, taking another piece of meat and throwing it a little closer to him.

The tabby lowered itself to the ground and took a few tentative steps toward the first piece of meat before stretching out its neck and delicately grabbing it.

"One piece down," whispered Jane.

Steve threw another piece, again landing it closer to the cat.

A few tentative steps and the second piece of meat was gone, but then it backed up a couple of paces, staring intently at Steve.

Another piece went toward the young cat. This time it stretched out its neck and sniffed at the tidbit, but didn't move closer.

Steve took a tentative step closer, then, putting down the plate, launched himself at the cat. He landed on top of it to a rousing chorus of screams, hissing, and spitting before the cat shot free and high-tailed it down the alley away from them.

"Ow!" said Steve loudly, rubbing at his lacerated hands as he picked himself up off the dirty alley. "Man, those claws are sharp! Are you sure getting feral cats is a good idea? I hate to think we'd be treated like that every time we went to feed them." He brushed futilely at the dirt and stains on his trousers.

Alan laughed. "You *jumped* on top of it… What did you expect it to do?"

"Well that didn't work," said Jane.

"That's not how to do it," said a voice from behind them. "It takes patience, sometimes weeks or months, to gain their trust, and then some never warm up to people and you have to let them go back on the streets after neutering them."

Jane swung round to see an older human woman in jeans and t-shirt standing there with a bag on her arm and a small pile of paper plates in her other hand.

"Who are you?"

"I'm Annie Subito. I feed the ferals here in this part of the alley," she said. "Someone has to look out for them and several of us do that by bringing water and food for them every day. Why are spacers like you trying to catch that youngster anyway? She's right skittish, only just got her coming for food. Likely your friend has set her back a month or two."

"We have a rodent problem," mumbled Jane.

"A what?" asked Annie. "You'll have to speak up, my hearing isn't as good as it was."

"A rodent problem on our ship," Jane repeated more loudly, going slightly red.

"Ah, then cats will help you put that to rights. Happens I have some needing homes. Teenagers like that one, not kittens. But they'll grow up in the ship and be at ease with it unlike older cats."

"You have?" said Alan, hopefully glancing at Jane. "Can we see them?"

"Sure you can. Just let me put the last of my food down for the ferals then I'll take you to my home."

"These ones you won't have to catch," she smiled as they neared a small row of cottages. "Their mothers are feral, but they're not now. They're used to being handled by all sorts of people, young and old, and even by my dog. But they've not seen ones like you," she said, looking sideways at Harran. "Not too many of you come to the Keissian port."

"No. We tend to trade further out," answered Harran. "There's a lot of cats around your home."

"Yes, they know they're welcome here and will get fed without me trying to bring them inside."

She led the way up the path through a small garden bordered by a couple of trees hung with wind chimes and spinners of every kind and hue.

"I like my garden," she said conversationally. "It creates gentle noise and color for me. Cats seem to like it too." She reached the doorway and turned to them. "Come on in, don't be shy. Nothing in here will claw or bite you. Talking of which I have some disinfectant wipes for those scratches of yours. Don't want them to go septic, especially as the alley is so dirty."

"Thank you," Steve said.

She led them into her front room, and gestured for them to sit down on one of the two sofas that took up most of the room. With a sharp bark, a shaggy black-and-white collie came running in to sniff the newcomers.

"You wait here and see the cats," said Annie. "I'll get the disinfectant." She walked out into the kitchen area as they took seats on the sofas.

Several cats had obviously made themselves at home, sitting on the back of one of the sofas and on a sideboard. One of the bolder ones, a fluffy tuxedo youngster, came strolling over to see them. Jane reached down and was rewarded with a touch by a cold, wet nose.

The young cat began to sniff her hand and gently rub his head against her.

"He's taken a shine to you, I see," said Annie as she came back with a couple of sealed wipes for Steve.

"Thanks," he said, breaking one open and wiping at the claw marks, a couple of which were fairly deep. He pocketed the other wipe. "I'll keep it for later."

Annie nodded and sat down beside Harran, who'd taken a seat alone on one of the sofas, letting the other three interact with the cats.

"Will he let me pick him up?" Jane asked, her voice gentle as she tentatively stroked the purring cat.

"Try him and see," Annie said. "As I said, all these in here have been socialized. How many cats are you looking for? I'd suggest at least two. I need to find homes for three of them otherwise they'll stay here with me and likely revert back to being feral. I do what I can, but I can't give them all a home."

Jane had picked up the fluffy one and was having a great time petting him as he turned round and round on her lap, his feathery black tail whisking itself just under her nose.

"That one's called Freddy," she said. "He's one I need to rehome. Good to see you're getting on well with him, I want them to go to a home where they aren't just work cats but are cared for as well. You'll get better results if you treat them like pets."

"What about the little grey one," Alan asked, pointing to a cat that had just walked in. "Is he looking for a home too?"

Annie reached out to pick up the grey one. "Yes, Smokey is. The third one is the tabby on the sideboard, another female like Smokey. I call her Ripples as her fur seems to be colored in ripples."

Smokey gave a glance at Harran and let out a hiss. Annie handed her off to Alan. "Seems they are wary of you Sholans," she said. "These cats came to me as kittens, brought by their mothers when they were just weaned. They dumped them in my living room then left as if to say they were my problem now! I've trapped many of the neighborhood cats and had them neutered and released them, keeping the few who were over-friendly and wanted to stay, but these two feral females — I think they are sisters — I just haven't been able to catch. They're too wily for my traps. So every kitten season I get a new batch of their babies to look after and find homes for."

"Surely they don't live too long outdoors on their own?" asked Steve, leaning over to pet the grey one.

"Oh they can live anything from three to ten years, but the indoors ones, or ones like these who are indoors at night, can live to be twenty."

"So they are well worth rehoming," said Jane. "We'd like these three then, if you're willing to sell them to us."

"I won't be selling them; you can have them. I'm just happy to find them what I'm sure will be a good home. You treat them right and make them feel wanted and loved, and when you stop at your merchant ports, they won't want to run off. And your rodent problem will be solved."

"I never thought of them trying to escape," said Harran. "We'll have to be careful the first few stops."

"How do you plan to take them to your ship? You can't bundle them up in a kit bag you know," Annie said, pointing at the bag which rested at Jane's feet. "I have a large cat basket you can use, since they're not very big yet. They'll all fit inside it just fine. You can send it back to me with a messenger."

"Are you sure we can't give you anything for them?" asked Steve.

"I'm sure. You'll need to go to the exotic pet store on the main walk and get supplies for them. A tray and cat litter for obvious reasons. You'll need to clean it every day and change it out every couple of weeks. Get dried cat food, they're used to it, and it is less messy than wet food. You can keep that for high days and holidays," she said, all business now. "Peter!" she called out. "Get me the large cat carrier from the shed, please."

"Yes, Gran," came the answer and in a few minutes a teenage boy arrived with a large carrier which he put behind the sofa where she sat.

"You found homes for them?" he asked.

"For the last three of them, yes," she said, getting up and going over to Alan to get the little grey cat.

"I opened it for you," said Peter.

"Thank you, dear," she said, going round to put Smokey into the carrier and shut the door. She went to Jane next and collected the long-haired cat. Finally she collected Ripples, who gave a meow of complaint as she was put into the carrier with the other two. "Ripples is a bit of a diva, standoffish like, but she'll get used to you."

"Uh, thank you," said Jane, gesturing to Steve as the strongest to take the carrier. "I'll see it gets back to you today."

'Just remember to give them time to adjust to their new home, now," Annie said as she led the way back to the door. "They're all neutered so worry of them having kittens. If you get a chance, next time you are at Alia, come and let me know how they're doing."

"We'll do that," said Harran as he stepped past her. "Thanks again. This was a lot easier than our futile attempts in the alley."

"There's always a right way to go about things," smiled Annie as she watched them leave.

They stowed the cat carrier in Jane's cabin and headed up to the crew's mess area, a small room with space for a table and bench seats as well as the obligatory stove and sink.

"You got what?" demanded John, their captain.

"Three cats. You know, furry critters that hunt mice and rats," said Alan.

"I know what cats are and what they do but why let another set of vermin free on the ship when we can't control the ones we have! You haven't let them loose have you?" he asked running his hand across his short, dark hair.

"No, they're in a carrier in my quarters," said Jane calmly.

"We could give them a try and if it doesn't work, we can find new homes for them. They're tame, not feral," said Steve.

"What have you got to say about it, Harran?" demanded John.

"I say it's worth a try," said Harran nonchalantly. "They were very well behaved when we saw them, and very affectionate. You could say they are a boost for morale on long trips."

"Morale boost be damned!"

"Let's face it, John, we won't have cats chewing on wiring or destroying other essential ship parts," said Jane in a conciliatory tone. "That's got to be better than we have now. Same with cargoes—no munching on them."

"That's surely a plus," said Steve, examining his scratches.

"How did you get those scratches if they are so tame, and how do we know this will work?" demanded John, frustrated, again running a hand through his hair.

"We don't, but I looked it up on my wrist comp on the way back, ancient people used the cats to protect their granaries from mice and rats. This isn't much different," said Jane.

"We tried to capture a feral one first," said Steve, "and it scratched me, it wasn't one of the three we have."

"You're in charge of them then," said John, pointing a finger at Jane. "I'm not having the ship smelling of dead vermin, you can all be responsible for looking after the cats and cleaning up after them!"

"Aye, sir," said Alan, squeezing off his bench seat.

"Where you going?" demanded John.

"To let the cats out so they can get accustomed to the ship."

"I'll come with you," said Jane, also getting up. "They *are* in my room."

"I'll see to sending the carrier back," said Harran, joining them.

"Go on, get out of here!" said John, gesturing in exasperation. "Just see we aren't drowning in cat fur! I'll not have them clogging up the air filters!"

A month later, Jane was sitting in the small mess with Freddy on her lap, petting him as he squirmed his way into a comfortable position. On the other side, Ripples was sniffing at Harran and letting him bend down to pet her.

"Well the vermin are certainly under control," said Alan from his seat. "And they leave them tidily near the airlock doors, so no problem with that. Seems like cats were the right way to go."

"Yes," said Jane. "Even John is getting used to them. I saw him giving Smokey a few treats the other day."

"Really? So much for his 'I'm having no other set of vermin loose on the ship' comment!" laughed Steve.

Meanwhile up on the flight deck, John stared intently at his monitor watching Smokey in the aft hold. On the screen, the cat stalked the aisle, staring fixedly into a dark shadow between two cargo crates.

The captain grinned and muttered encouragement as Smokey's butt began to wiggle, slowly at first, then with increased energy just before she pounced into the shadow. Moments later she emerged with a dead rodent held in her mouth, one almost as big as her. He cheered as she strutted off toward the airlock.

In the mess, they'd heard the captain's voice over the comm. "Yes! You go, kitty! Well done!"

Jane grinned, giving Freddie extra pets. "Looks like the cats are a unanimous addition to the crew."

Ripley

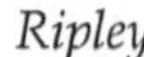

THE STINKIEST FISH
James W. Bates

IF YOU GO TO ANY THESAURUS WEBSITE AND SEARCH, THE TERM, "A FISH Story" is defined as 'an extravagant or incredible tale.' Well, I'm here to relate a story involving fish that imparts hard-earned wisdom and very simple advice. You're reading this book, which means you're interested in helping stray and feral cats. But doing your part may seem a bit daunting because catching street-smart and/or wild creatures can be easier said than done. Allow me to humbly share five words that got me from points A to B on my first kitty safari — "Use the stinkiest fish possible!"

I grew up a "dog person" in suburban Southern New Jersey. My family had many pets but it wasn't until my post-college, back-in-the-nest years that a cat entered my life. Benjamin Franklin Cat was a watermelon-shaped striped stray that adopted my parents. He was a gregarious fellow that put me to mind of late-in-life Orson Welles. He took advantage when food was readily available and abundant. But for the purpose of this piece, the important fact about Ben is that he was an indoor/outdoor cat that could take care of himself but chose to join a kind family. Before life's path led me out of the nest and to Hollywood, Ben convinced me that cats are cool.

Apartment living in Southern California became my new reality. Circumstances like renting rules, the lack of a yard, and work schedules meant that getting a dog was out of the question. A few years later my fiancé moved across country to live with me and along with her came her indoor-only, grumpy cat — Miss Audrey. My new furry roommate remained loyally attached to my wife. I accepted I would never be the apple of this cat's eye but quickly came to love her. Then my career shifted to 'work from home' and I learned the true wonders of sharing your daily life with a cat. And when Audrey passed peacefully, I couldn't wait more than a few months until we adopted a cat to fill the void. Mithril, the saddest looking cat at the shelter, joined us in the apartment. We both loved her, but much like Audrey, she preferred my wife to me.

Ten years into my-work-from-home era, circumstances allowed us to buy a house. This is a huge deal in Southern California. My wife maintained a steady career but for me this was defying the odds, and even as the head writer of the number-one kids' action show in the world the best we could swing was a modest house in what's considered a Class-B area. Mithril loved the added living space and we soon found ourselves rescuing yet another cat—the super friendly and amazingly photogenic Oberon. My new buddy was just that—we really connected! While I spent fifty to seventy hours a week in my home office, he was always there next to my keyboard. The Bates home now housed two cats and my non-stop social media posts (mostly Oberon pictures) solidified my growing reputation as a Crazy Cat Daddy. From Poe to Steinbeck to Hemingway… "Writers and cats" are a well-documented phenomena but my experience was evolving. I'd eventually prove that being a feline-loving writer does not automatically make you a rugged hunter like Hemingway.

The house was a sixty-year-old rancher that had plenty of character but its one real selling point was the quirky, walled-in backyard. The majority of the lot's space was taken up by a nice in-ground pool but there were also a number of exotic trees that reminded us of Jurassic Park. We could sit in the roofed-in patio and read or just lounge about. The comfy confines were also a prime spot to observe an added bonus to our suburban paradise—the community cats! Harkening back to my old New Jersey area, this neighborhood's suburban qualities were much more feral- and stray-cat populated than the higher traffic area in which our apartment was located. I learned interesting truths about community strays, TNR programs, and ferals. It also was immediately clear that our new yard was a safe-haven with its walls and a kitty oasis with its pool full of freely available water. Cats would come and go but there was one that basically came with the house. We learned from neighbors that this inherited yard cat had been named Daisy. We hadn't named Mithril or Oberon but both their shelter-given names were literary allusions and so we found Daisy's name fitting since my wife and I are big *Great Gatsby* fans.

Over the next few years, I would flirt with the idea of bringing Daisy in but she was a long-time feral. She'd look through windows into our house and occasionally interact with our inside cats. She'd 'hang out' in the yard and once flopped down just ten feet away from me as I read on the patio. Sadly, she never quite became comfortable enough with me to have a chance to join our family. For the four years that Daisy was a part of our eco-system, I put out food and water for her even though she was "not our cat." I eventually accepted that this was the extent of our relationship but I didn't mind sharing the uneaten expensive kibble that our spoiled insiders leftover each morning. I eventually started buying separate, less fancy bags just to put outside. Then one day—Daisy stopped showing up.

A hard reality here is that as friendly as our neighborhood is to wild kitties, there are cars and coyotes. Life expectancy is short for ferals and strays because of the dangers of living outside. The local policy of shelters and rescues is that you must agree that adoptees be "indoors only." Wistfully, I continued to put out the bowls of kibble but one way or another Daisy had moved on. Her absence opened the territory for someone new—enter Bubba! This newcomer was an eye-catchingly handsome critter with a tortoise shell coat and white feet. What it had in looks it lacked in gymnastic skill but the goofball never let an occasional slip off a tree branch deter it. I had kept up my kibble-sharing schedule and before long Bubba became my friendly patio-reading companion. Those first summer months lead me to two discoveries—Calicos are almost always genetically female and the notch in Bubba's ear was a sign that the fixing had already been done. A third discovery fully thrust me into Cat Daddy territory and that was SHE was very friendly and thus probably an abandoned stray. In short order, she was sitting on the patio couch with me and was given a new name. Long story short, my wife honored the lost Daisy by giving our new "Not Our Cat" a Gatsby-inspired name – West Egg. (It's a location in the novel.)

West Egg continued to make it clear she was not going anywhere. Dog-like in her desire for attention and approval, she communicated with endearing vocalizations that were funny "mwars" that reminded me of Edward G Robinson. My bonding with Oberon had been a revelation in my cat-centric life and now I had a second cat sharing affection I never knew I needed. Yet, we already had two cats. There were a few half-hearted attempts to get her adopted to a different home but it was clear she wasn't going anywhere but into my house. Bringing in West Egg meant she needed a clean bill of health from a vet.

So… I had to catch her. How hard could that be? West Egg was so friendly. She approached and demanded petting, was a huge fan of treats, and actively wanted me on the patio to hang out. I grew confident that when the time came, that I could simply scoop her up… but I was wrong. Her natural defensive instincts made attempts to grab her akin to an old-timey greased pig catchin' contest. She remained sweet and trusting after our "cat and schmuck" games and I figured she just considered my clumsy attempts were playtime but I feared I'd lose her trust before actually snatching her.

I needed a new plan. I would stop my aggressive grabbing efforts and try logic. Cats love boxes! My initial idea was to leave out the cardboard box cat carrier we got from the shelter. It was a box and maybe she'd just climb in and allow me to close it. That didn't work and so I tried putting her bowl of kibble in the carrier but she didn't fall for it. After a couple of days, I placed the bowl back in its regular spot so she wouldn't starve. I gave up on the carrier plan and went to the internet for advice. That's when I learned about the commercially available Have-A-Heart traps. I then surfed neighborhood information web boards and found a stranger with a trap that she was willing to lend me. Plan C was in play! In theory, the borrowed spring-loaded trap would do all the work and then even serve as a kitty carrier. The hardest part would be getting a scheduled appointment at the Pet Doctors. Ah… again, I had no clue.

There is an African proverb, "Until the lion learns how to write, every story will glorify the hunter." I can't play it that way. Can't claim to be John Patterson quarrelling with the Man-Eaters of Tsavo. Put me in the Wiley E. Coyote 'Super Genius' category. I accidentally activated the spring on that Have-A-Heart so many times I'm lucky to still have fingers. But now I will repay you for reading the details of my journey with the surefire way to lure any cat… yes, finally! On to the Fish Story!

Once I managed to get the trap engaged, I needed bait. First, I tried her normal kibble in a bowl but she cautiously resisted. My second attempt was to up the game and put out some wet food. I put a scoop of the pâté I give my inside cats within the trap. I later found evidence that West Egg was intrigued enough to jostle the trap and knock over the bowl. Yet my foil avoided going in. I resorted to a deeper web search and found someone who baited with Kentucky Fried Chicken. Always happy to find an excuse to visit the Colonel, I procured some juicy Original Recipe. Alas, even food I can't resist was not a recipe for success and West Egg did not enter the trap.

I reached a cartoonish level of frustration. I'd call and check in with the vets to see if they might be able to see me IF I caught this silly beast. I again began to worry about losing West Egg's trust. But I couldn't expect to keep the borrowed trap indefinitely so I pressed on. Cartoons are what I write for a living, Wile E. Coyote was who I had become and so why not go super simple with what toons taught us as kids — all felines love fish! My inside cats did love a small taste of tuna whenever we made sandwiches. Maybe tuna could end my two-week safari? I confidently placed a portion of canned tuna in the trap and waited but by day's end — West Egg had resisted!

More research followed. I kept finding the same techniques that had failed for me. Then I saw a tidbit about how cats were often drawn to the smelliest varieties and brands of wet food. Scent inducement led even finicky eaters to their bowls. Inspired, I forwent canned pâté and subtle tuna and hunted down something really smelly! I perused the supermarket aisles and found the canned mackerel. I like seafood. Canned tuna has a spot in my rotation of preferred eats, a good Caesar Salad dressing featuring anchovies works well for me, but I had never experienced the magnificent pungency of canned mackerel. The odor emitted and aura created as I opened the can evoked memories of the villains removing the lid of the Ark of the Covenant in *Raiders*.

Desperate but hopeful, I placed the stinky bait and went inside. I had not even settled into a chair before I heard the triumphant snap of the trap! With wonder, I peeked at the patio and there was West Egg safely secured in the Have-A-Heart! There was one comical hitch to my victory and that was that in the process of exuberantly getting to the fish, or in her startled reaction, West Egg had thrashed about. She was drenched in mackerel juice! But a smelly car ride and an added vet fee for a bath were a nominal price to pay for this hunter bagging his elusive prey! She was declared very healthy for a stray and checked for a chip to make sure there was no owner searching for her. She moved in that night, integrated with her new family, and has owned the house.

Since West Egg moved in eight and a half years ago, many community cats have found safe haven in our backyard. Most just pass through but one tabby has also been brought in thanks to stinky mackerel. When a couple of needy ginger ferals appeared, I reached out to a neighborhood friend who had "cat colony status" and a hook up with a TNR organization. With my experience and allies, between 2020 and 2025, I have trapped and TNR'd half a dozen ferals. Four of them live out back and enjoy multiple daily feedings. A few of them could instantly join the family and excel as insiders but my cat-loving but sane wife has made the math clear, "One more cat moving inside equals one husband moving outside."

Community cats continue to come and go and there may be more hunting in my Cat Daddy future. If that is the case, I am up for the task. And you can be too. If you have a feral you want to adopt, TNR, or just help, don't be intimidated. You can do it if you remember to use the *stinkiest* fish possible!

West Egg, covered in mackerel juice on her gotcha day.

TRADITION

Patrick Thomas

As the sun soared high above the clouds in the midday sky, a despairing few were forced onto the field of the Coliseum. The wretched procession served only to remind the assembled that the heyday of the games was long past, as was the Empire. In times gone by, crowds filled the stadium to capacity and beyond. No longer. Only the combatants and a few meager handfuls watched these games. The bars the Rome city government placed at all entrances saw to that. Only a select few were allowed to visit, and then only at certain times. It was simplicity itself to plan the games around this schedule. During all other times, none save the congregation were capable of entry. They and theirs had been doing it since the Coliseum was erected. Some even remembered that day.

Traditions were passed down from generation to generation, through both word and action. Of course, differences evolved over the centuries. They always do. The modern games saw both combatants and spectators wearing no clothes. Only the Emperor was allowed a crown of olive leaves to denote her station. Out of respect for tradition, male and female rulers alike were addressed as Emperor. Naturally, both sexes participated fully in the games. Some of the best gladiators were female. Water games were only possible after great rains since the mechanisms which had flooded the arena were destroyed ages before. Even if they were not, the lake on which it was built had long been dried to a puddle.

Today's warriors went into the ring weaponless, using only wits and skill to survive. Sometimes it sufficed. Often it did not. Most modern gladiators had certain genetic advantages over their opponents. Since they ran the games, this was not questioned. At least not for long.

Every game needs its grunts, a fodder class to enable warriors to slaughter a superior number of foes triumphantly for the thrill of the crowd. These games were no different. Fodder did not know how to fight and were shown only the very basics of combat. This suited the game masters. As a rule, the grunts were puny so that even the lowest gladiator was assured victory. It kept the warriors from grumbling too loudly.

Soon the warm sun would shine its last upon the seven who stood on that field of battle, that pasture of death. Instructions were given and followed. As one, the condemned marched before the Emperor and saluted, chanting "We who are about to die salute you!" And so the tradition was kept.

During the pomp and ceremony, one grunt saw his chance, possibly the last he would ever be given. Taking it without hesitation, he broke away from his guards and quickly vanished between a crack, his thin tail the last of him to vanish. The ruins provided him with a temporary haven. Furious that her will had been thwarted, the Emperor ordered the grunt be recaptured. The guards began the search immediately. It might take days, but he would be found, or the guards would take his place. The Emperor had never been a pleasant one to work for.

Those grunts that remained were herded together in the center. A single group made a much neater target than six little ones. The gladiator moved toward them slowly, his head held high and a swagger in his steps. Watching, the assembled could not help but be reminded of Christians being thrown to a lion. The six trembled before the gladiator. The smell of their fear flowed over his nostrils, awakening primal instincts. The scent excited him. He could almost savor the sweet taste of blood as he eagerly moved in for the kill.

The crowd hushed in anticipation of the slaughter to come. They knew this gladiator. He was a favorite son and none who watched him ever came away disappointed, save his opponents. Them he toyed with, building the crowds' emotions up into a frenzy so they experienced the ecstasy of the kill vicariously.

The battle was good. One grunt died right off. Her eyes showed only surprise as her body no longer responded to her commands. Or perhaps it was shock at how her blood made the ground an even prettier shade of crimson or how badly her bowels smelled outside of her body. None of these thoughts ever crossed the gladiator's mind as he moved on toward his next kill. Two grunts, one male and the other female, were immobilized by the gladiator stunning, then sitting on them.

The remaining three, too terrified to run out of his reach, remained as still as statues. After partaking of some sport, the gladiator slew two with fang and claw without even bothering to get up. Rising to his feet, the gladiator turned his tender attention toward the two grunts trapped beneath him. Both attempted flight. One was dead before he took five steps. The other was lifted and dangled above the gladiator's head. A vision of the gaping maw of the gladiator was all the grunt saw as he was suspended above the sharp, white fangs, glistening with saliva. The crowd went mad with delight at each squirm. The gladiator lowered and raised the grunt, dangling his face in the jaws of sudden death. Instead of freezing, he struck back, slashing at the gladiator's eye. The grunt drew blood. The shock of the gladiator was replaced by anger, as he literally saw red. Lowering the grunt down for the final time, he closed his mighty jaws around his opponent's neck. He did not let up until he heard the snap. The crowd stomped their approval.

One lone survivor still stood. Larger than the others, she massed less than half of what the gladiator did. She would not die easily, if at all. The last grunt drew courage from the thick red liquid flowing down the gladiator's face. He bled. The gladiator was mortal. He could die. Perhaps at her hand.

The final combat lasted several minutes, far longer than the sum of her compatriots' combined time. Almost as long as the last gladiator he faced. Unheard of for a grunt. What she lacked in skill and strength she made up for with heart and treachery. Her valiant efforts wounded the gladiator until he moved with a limp and his hind leg poured crimson.

Sadly, in this battle, heart was not enough. In succession, three blows were struck to head, chest, and gut. The grunt was brought down. In the heat of battle, the gladiator was barely able to keep his warrior's frenzy in check. He remembered tradition with less than a heartbeat to spare.

A valiant fighter received a voting chance. The crowd signified their choices, but the final decision lay with the Emperor. Limb extended, she popped a single claw parallel to the ground. The she-rat's eyes burned bright with the light of hope. It was quickly extinguished as the feline Emperor turned the digit downward. The killing blow was struck without hesitation.

The gladiator had never doubted the outcome. The Emperor freed only one in five hundred and never on a day such as today. Today the Emperor was hungry.

That was another change. The fallen of the games were often consumed by the victor. After the Emperor had been given her pick from the corpses, of course. Her latest meal was the brave she-rat, chosen not by her courage but by her size. The gladiator placed the carcass before the Emperor. This time, she popped all ten claws, lowered her face, and devoured her fill. When the black cat raised her bloody jaws minutes later, the she-rat was bare of flesh save for the head. That belonged to the gladiator, a trophy to his prowess. He may make it a gift to his human family, although they would not appreciate it for what it was.

Many feasted that day as the gladiator was generous with his kills. He even offered to share with the black crow who often sat beside the Emperor. Out of range of claw and fang, of course. The offer was greeted with a flutter of wings as the crow landed at the black cat's side. His fellows also flew down from their perches and, following their commander's lead, took up positions near the contingent of cats, but well out of reach. Gladiators all they might be, but that did not mean they trusted each other.

Even now, tradition was observed.

"Hail, Nero," said the crow.

"Hail, Augustus," returned the tabby. "Ready for some sport?"

"Ready as ever," spoke the crow, not nearly as enthusiastically as his fellow. Augustus had never shared his companion's blood lust. He was still made nervous by the way the cat longingly stared at the matches beneath her throne. Nor were his fears made any easier by the cat's insistence that they be by her side at all times. The crow knew her well and did not trust her present impotence to keep her desires reigned in. It had not in the past. The crow recalled the first time. And the last. It had occurred in the distant land of Chicago, in the Emperor's bovine incarnation. Still, he did nothing. He was not Emperor this time. Nero was. Preferring to reflect on more pleasant matters. he returned the cat's question.

"And thou?"

"As you say, I am as ready as ever," the cat said. The crow cawed loudly. The sound was very much like the sound of a full-grown man's laugh coming out of the mouth of a crying babe.

"Are thou sure? Accepting these morsels without having to work has added much weight to your belly," said the crow, stepping back three paces as he did so.

"True," said the cat. "But I am still the best gladiator here." And the crow nodded because it was true. The black cat was deadly and, unlike most felines, remembered to fight dirty.

The Emperor allowed the crowd time to finish feasting before calling forth the next sport. A mighty black Labrador Retriever, a coarse rope around his neck, was dragged forth onto the field. A dozen cats were doing the leading. They paused while his crimes were read before the assemblage. For rabble-rousing, attempting to organize the strays (dog, cat, bird, and rodent alike) that lived outside the Coliseum and, most importantly, for subversion of the Emperor's will, the sentence was death. What was not announced was that he almost succeeded and had come very close to causing the black cat's death. The sentence was to be carried out immediately.

The canine's life did not come cheaply. Within seconds, five cats lay wounded or dead.

The Emperor called in the air support, but the birds waited for a nod from the crow before joining the fray. Multitudes of assorted birds swooped down upon the dog, intent on putting out his eyes. It worked well enough to throw him off balance and allow two cats to leap on his back. Turning to block off further attack, he was stopped by the shock of recognition at one of the feline gladiators. It was a trusted lieutenant.

"Et tu?" he asked. The cat hung his head for a moment as if in shame, then leapt to join his fellows on the canine's back.

On the sideline, the Emperor looked nervously at the crow by his side. The crow returned his look with a questioning glance.

"I half expect you to go to his aid," spoke the black cat. The crow let out a sigh.

"No. I learned my lesson after my third lifetime. For things ordained, vengeance makes little sense," said the crow sagely. The cat nodded, for this was also true.

Meanwhile, the black dog had been brought low. The Emperor made a demand of the dog's former lieutenant.

"Brutus, bring me his head."

With great time and effort, it was done. The head was placed before the Emperor on a newspaper that had blown in from the street outside.

The date read March 14.

In the distance, a mockingbird yelled "Beware...".

The games continued through the day. Gladiators fought, won, and lost. Some gained glory, while others breathed their last. During the closing ceremonies, a man in overalls entered the arena. He cast stones at warriors and spectators alike. Several died from their wounds. It was a common occurrence, and the Emperor was content to let it go. That is until a rock came too close and gave her a glancing blow. It was thus that her wraith was incurred. All gladiators were ordered to attack the man. They did. The man would have defeated one, perhaps even a dozen, but there were far more than that. The cats bit and raked his skin as the birds pecked at his eyes and groin. Soon, the man was unable to see. The reason for this was plain. The crow was feasting on his eyeball, savoring the jelly-like flesh. The man tried to run but tripped over the black cat who had blocked his escape. Falling into a drainage rut, the human smashed his skull and spine. Either was a serious injury. Together, they spelled his death.

The Emperor declared the games ended and told all to stay away for many days. For safety's sake, she said. After all but the crow had gone, she crept down into the rut and began picking at the body. The crow, in shock, dropped the remaining vitreous humor from his beak and flew off quickly. The black cat had clawed open a pocket and now held a lighter in her teeth. The familiar look burned brightly in her eyes.

Having taken to the air, his wings did their best to put as much distance between himself, the black cat, and the personal tradition that was sure to follow. In his mind, he could already hear the sirens and feel the flames.

His absence would be temporary. The black crow would return. They all would. The games would continue as long as Rome stood. Perhaps even longer. Tradition demanded it.

Molly

MYSTERIOUS ANGEL
Rigel Ailur

THE MYSTERIOUS FELINE WITH TWO TAILS APPEARED ABOUT SEVEN MONTHS ago on the waning edge of winter. Since then, she'd roamed the tree-lined neighborhood, always alone and afraid, availing herself of the food and water set out by various people but never trusting any of the humans.

The stealth cat proved to be so elusive, Alex wondered if anyone else had gotten a good look at her at all. If so, surely the Two-Tailed Cat would have been the talk of the neighborhood — likely to her detriment.

Alex had kept waiting for the notoriety to surface but, to her great relief, it never did.

"Good morning, Little One. How are you today?" Standing at the top of the three stairs leading down from the covered porch, Alex leaned a bit over the cast-iron railing. She spoke softly to the living shadow lurking below among the roses surrounding the house.

The tortie cat didn't answer. She never did.

Pre-dawn grey concealed the cat from all but the sharpest eyes, but Alex could tell exactly where she hunkered down just clear of the rose bushes' thorns.

Early morning dew made the sweet fragrance of the plants that much stronger. A multitude of rainbow blooms remained, but before long, autumn frosts would trigger the plants' dormancy.

The cat's fear, extreme but not feral, told Alex she'd been dumped. But — at least with regard to Alex — the cat no longer fled at top speed. The terror had given way to extreme skittishness, to milder anxiety, to distrust, to haughty avoidance just on principle.

Alex had occasionally glimpsed her in daylight. She had plentiful orange streaks through her short coat, especially on her face, so in good light no one would mistake her for a black cat. But in the pre-dawn gray, the predominant black of the fur ensured she blended perfectly in all but the faintest shadows.

The feline gazed up at Alex pressing against the rail to better see her, then sauntered unconcernedly away around the house toward the back.

She moved with the same feline grace she'd exhibited ever since Alex had first noticed her. Since then, the cat had accepted only the food and water Alex left out and had rebuffed all her offers of shelter. Thanks to Alex and other neighbors, the feline had looked sleek and fairly well fed despite living outside.

At least at first.

The kitty hadn't lost her dedication to the outdoors, but late in summer she had lost her sleekness. The bulge of gestating kittens had taken care of that.

Until now. Now most of the bulge had vanished, replaced only by the swell of plentiful milk.

Time to discover where the mysterious furball disappeared to. Alex had waited as long as she dared. Now that the little tortie was—obviously—no longer pregnant, Alex needed to find the kittens. A colony in the neighborhood wouldn't be good for anyone, not for the cats and not for the wildlife.

Treading lightly, this time Alex trailed after her without crowding her. She avoided the thorns by giving the rose bushes along the side of the house a wide berth. Her furry friend did the same.

The cat paused and cast a suspicious look back at her follower.

Alex kept her distance, assuring the fluff she intended no harm to her or her new family.

The cat remained unconvinced.

Suddenly bursting into a sprint, she tore off across the lawn and into a neighbor's backyard as fast as her four paws could carry her.

Alex sighed, remaining perfectly still.

She waited.

So much life everywhere, all around. Finding several tiny kittens wouldn't be easy.

The wind came and went, rustling the fall leaves on the trees and sending even more of them swirling to the ground. The air stilled, just for a few brief instants, and Alex heard what she'd hoped for.

Mewling.

Barely audible, so incredibly faint she nearly missed it.

Then another gust obliterated the silence. The gale whistled through trees and brought the strong scent of the pines mingled with that of the oaks, birches, and locust trees. The smell of impending rain mixed with the scents of pine and roses. Heavy cloud cover obscured the sunrise and lengthened the morning twilight. All in all, a brisk autumn day.

An excellent day to get newborn kittens out of the cold and damp and into a warm, cozy house.

The mother cat had streaked off to the right. Alex strode in the opposite direction, her steps sloshing more than crackling on the soggy leaves and pine needles on her neighbor's normally pristine lawn. The next lot with the dilapidated two-story house posed a stark contrast to the otherwise tidy neighborhood.

The house virtually abandoned, its owner had died a few years back. Someone mowed the grass once or twice a summer, but otherwise the place reeked of desertion.

Filthy siding was warping and starting to pull away from the wooden frame. Ivy clinging to one corner of the structure was spreading and showed no indication of relinquishing its claim.

A section of the roof had buckled and was on the verge of caving in completely.

Thank heavens the fluff hadn't chosen that hazard as her lair.

The aluminum shed in the back didn't look any better, but at least it posed no danger of collapsing in on itself. Eying it, Alex estimated she could barely stand upright in it without hitting her head. Considering her tiny stature, and that the shed measured only about four foot by four foot, she wondered why the people had bothered.

Dirt and grime had clogged the track and cemented the doors in position, making them nearly impossible to move. Alex gripped one door and heaved.

Emitting a teeth-gnashing screech Alex hoped the whole neighborhood didn't hear, the door gave way and slid a foot to the side.

Alex peered into the blackness and willed her eyes to adjust. Indistinct shapes clarified in the gloom. Alex hadn't expected much, and she'd guessed correctly. An empty metal gas can. Some old-style window screens leaning against one wall. A pile of ancient rags in the back corner.

Rags that moved.

Alex took off her favorite Steelers' sweatshirt and slung it over one shoulder. Then she went and very gingerly started sorting through the material, which looked like old towels. Although filthy, at least they'd remained dry.

A spider or two, harmless ones, skittered off as Alex peeled away the last rags. Five tiny bodies squirmed and cried piteously.

Holding her sweatshirt as best as she could with one hand, she transferred the babies into it. Their high-pitched 'yowls' intensified. Alex had to smile. Good lungs. Strong, healthy kittens. Not that she wanted to alarm them, but their energy pleased her.

Mother cat hissed and snarled at Alex from the doorway. Back arched, both tails straight up, every hair on her body stood on end, she looked like she weighed thirty pounds instead of ten.

"It's all right," Alex spoke soothingly. "I'm helping you. Come with me." Taking great care with her precious bundle, Alex got to her feet. "Come on. I promise you, it's ok."

The tortie stood her ground, growling even more loudly and making a vicious swiping motion with one paw, claws fully extended.

Still speaking in calming, conciliatory tones, Alex took another step. She wondered if she would need to nudge the protective parent to one side — and if her legs would get shredded when she did so.

To Alex's immense relief, the cat gave way and decided not to maul her. Emitting low warning sounds the entire way, the feline followed Alex back to her front porch and inside. Alex eased the front door shut with one foot.

Her front door opened into the split-level house's landing. Six stairs on the right went down to the game room with its fireplace and bar, and to the laundry room and garage. Six on the left led upstairs to the rest of the house, including the bedrooms.

Alex went up the stairs, with the kitchen straight ahead and the living room and dining area to her left. Turning down the hallway to the right, Alex went into the closest bedroom. Once the furious mother feline came in, she shut that door as well.

She sat down on the floor, opening the sweatshirt in her lap to examine the kittens. The tortie's complaints subsided even more.

The five wriggling balls of fur had stopped crying. Two torties, a gray tabby, an orange tabby, and a black and white, all with umbilical cords still attached. Eyes not yet open, but mouths open just fine as they searched for their meal. Paws, toes, tails (one apiece), everything looked simply perfect.

They looked fairly clean, and free of fleas—probably due to the cold weather. Alex would make sure, regarding eliminating fleas and any other parasites as well, but so far, so good.

Alex slid the sweatshirt off her lap and onto the plush purple carpeting toward the mother. Then she slid back until she leaned against the wall and waited.

The bedroom held one double bed and two dressers—both empty. She didn't use it at all and almost never had houseguests. Consequently, the space didn't contain much of anything, let alone anything that could hurt the cats, or that they could destroy.

The mother cat hissed a few times at Alex for good measure and even gave another air-swat. Then she examined her brood, nudging and grooming each one of them. Satisfied Alex hadn't harmed them, the mother stretched out on the sweatshirt, eying Alex fiercely the whole time.

The kittens clustered around her tummy and soon nursed contentedly.

Once they were done, the tortie would want a good, secure, hiding spot for her little ones. Alex reached over and opened the closet door a few inches. She'd already stacked blankets in one corner, and in the opposite corner she had a plastic box lid, its lip only an inch high, with some litter in it. The babies wouldn't need it right away, but she wanted it there for them.

A full-sized litter box sat across the room on the other side of the bed for the mother cat. On the same side of the room where Alex sat, she'd placed a drinking water fountain up on the dresser, along with a bowl of dry cat food. Kitten chow, since the mother needed the extra nourishment.

Alex's kitchen contained plenty of canned food, stocked up for just such a circumstance, same with the dry food and the litter. After she was certain her houseguests would stay calm, she'd go open a can.

In the meantime, Alex rested her back against the wall and listened to the gurgling of the fountain. Soon, the tortie started purring.

Alex released a huge sigh of contentment.

Finally, a breakthrough.

Alex didn't sense any more fear or hostility from the cat. She still radiated wariness, but the dam of distrust had broken. Alex expected swift progress to follow.

Eventually she'd need to decide what to do next.

The cats could stay indefinitely. Alex could easily care for them and had no one else at home to consider.

She loved cats. Yet she wondered if someone who didn't work all day like she normally did could give them even more attention and affection.

Regardless, no rush. In any case, they weren't going anywhere until after the kittens were weaned.

And thanks to being able to write any place she liked, Alex didn't have to go anywhere either.

By the time Alex stood and stretched, sunlight streamed in the window. She estimated that a few hours had passed, making it around ten o'clock.

The mother feline lifted her head and shot Alex a measuring look before relaxing. She still reclined on the gold Steelers sweatshirt. The pile of kittens had fallen asleep against her. They didn't stir as Alex slipped out of the room.

After lunch, Alex peeked in and found her sweatshirt abandoned. She tiptoed to the closet, the door still only inches ajar. Despite the deep gloom, Alex saw the whole family of cats slumbering among the blankets. How did the purring not wake them?

She refilled the nearly-empty food, made sure the fountain had plenty of water, then left the kitties to their most urgent business.

Cat napping was really hard work.

After giving them the first day to settle in, Alex started sleeping in that bedroom as well. She enjoyed the companionship every bit as much as they did.

Alex swore she could see them getting bigger by the day, if not by the hour. They grew in leaps and bounds.

And in no time, that's exactly what they were doing: leaping and bounding everywhere in their bedroom.

She kept the door shut since she hadn't yet cat-proofed the rest of the house. She kept meaning to, but some instinct she couldn't explain told her they wouldn't be staying.

They sometimes still retreated to the closet, but just as often, Alex found them in the patch of sunlight wherever it hit the bed.

Of course she named them. She couldn't very well keep thinking of them merely as 'Tortie' and 'Tabby'.

She christened the mother cat Teyla. The name suited the feline's warrior mother instinct. Alex marveled at the dexterity of both tails and estimated that Teyla couldn't be much older than two.

The baby torties, she named Kira and Aeryn. Kira's fur showed as much red as black. Aeryn, on the other hand, sported mostly black coloring with a few orange and white patches, mostly on her face and stomach.

After considerable pondering, Alex settled on Jinn, Brisco, and Starbuck for the black and white, the gray tabby, and the orange tabby, respectively.

It bothered Alex not at all to spend the bulk of the day keeping them company. When she wasn't playing with them, she'd sprawl out on the bed and catch up on her reading. Or she'd use an antique breakfast-in-bed stand, the miniature table kind one put on the bed over one's legs, and work on her laptop.

With great satisfaction, she typed the last few sentences of the penultimate chapter. Once she finished the next one, she'd send the manuscript to her editor a whole two weeks early.

Editors liked that.

And not just editors. Alex also considered it cause for celebration.

If only she could move without disturbing so many.

Brisco and Starbuck perched on each of her shoulders. Kira, on the tray right next to the laptop, alternated between snoozing and helping to type. Teyla had wedged herself on Alex's lap under the table, along with Aeryn.

After closing the laptop, she leaned back into a stack of pillows. The kittens adjusted their positions, moving from her shoulders and tucking themselves under her chin where they promptly resumed snoring.

White-and-black Jinn, the rebel, remained aloof and lounged luxuriously on the dresser. Occasional yawns punctuated his supremely contented purrs.

Thinking '*if you can't beat them…*' she closed her eyes and prepared to join them in their slumber.

She had no plans for that Thursday afternoon.

At persistent meowing, Alex opened one eye.

Teyla stood over the food bowl and rebuked Alex sternly at its horrifying condition.

Smirking, Alex gently relocated the kittens from on top of her to the bed. Plenty of food remained in the half-full bowl.

"All right, you are eating it faster, I'll give you that."

Teyla meowed again.

"Yes, I know. It's time for the good stuff. I'll be right back."

Alex went to the kitchen for the wet kitten chow. She got two cans from one cupboard and clean bowls from another.

They still nursed, but last week the kittens had started investigating, then eating, the canned food. Now, at four weeks going on five, they also ate some of the dry food.

None of the feline crew hesitated to express extreme disapproval when either was unavailable.

Alex plopped the canned food on the plates, balanced them in one hand, then returned to the furballs' room.

They'd all jumped onto the dresser and eagerly awaited her serving them dinner.

As they happily devoured their feast, Alex got the bag of dry food from the drawer and topped off that dish as well.

At the distinctive engine rattle of a car driving by outside, Alex paused a beat before closing the drawer. She'd heard that same car twice before in the last half hour. This time it idled either right out front or not more than a house or two away, accompanied by a bell-like chime.

Teyla jerked upright, head whipping around. Completely forgetting the food, the little cat sprang from the dresser to the bed then up onto the windowsill.

She meowed insistently and increasingly loudly, her agitation growing as she prowled back and forth in front of the window. The two tails whipped in agitation.

The bell repeated, and Teyla yowled even louder.

Leaving the cats in their room, Alex dashed out front. An old model Buick, baby blue, parked on the opposite side of the road, driver's door open and engine running and still pinging away.

A young woman, likely not more than thirty and dressed in cerulean sweats, stood a few yards away frantically shaking some metal wind chimes and trying to look every which way at once. Short, disheveled hair added to the youthful appearance.

Tears streamed down her face, and blotches of angry red color in her cheeks marred her pale complexion.

Alex already knew the answer, but she asked anyway. "Are you all right? Can I help you?"

The woman jumped as if shot, then wiped at her face and tried in vain to compose herself as the words rushed out of her between sobs.

"My ex stole my cat… dumped her. Maybe near here. His sister lives close… She just told me…" She swallowed air and scrubbed her face again.

"It's been nearly a year," she managed only slightly more evenly. "I tried everything. Called the police and all the shelters. Even all the other vets I know. I've been searching.

"But I live two hours from here. And I just found out she might be around here. It's a longshot, but she always loved these chimes. She played with them all the time. And she'd come running when they made noise."

"She heard." Alex pointed up at the window to where Teyla still ran back and forth. "Come on in."

For just a moment, Alex thought the woman's knees would buckle. Instead she managed to follow Alex inside and into the cats' room.

The moment Alex opened the door, Teyla bounded down onto the bed then launched herself into the woman's arms. The purring sounded like a jet engine. The cat clung and rubbed her head all over the woman's face, neck, and shoulders.

"Something tells me she missed you," Alex said, a wry smile on her face. "Just a little, maybe."

"She looks so wonderful! Thank you so much for taking care of her! I– She had babies!"

Alex chuckled at the woman's belated observation. Indeed, the five pairs of inquisitive eyes watched her every move quite closely as she wiped her face then blew her nose and crammed the Kleenex back in her pocket.

Then Alex grew serious. "You're obviously mutually overjoyed at the reunion. I'm so happy for both of you."

"I can't thank you enough. I was beside myself." She stroked and hugged Teyla who was still snuggling against her. "She looks wonderful. And so do all the kittens."

Alex grinned as the woman's professional habits asserted themselves.

She set Teyla on the dresser and, after using a tiny bottle of hand sanitizer from her other pocket, gave the feline a careful looking over. Then she examined each and every little one in turn.

"Perfect health," the woman declared. "I'm Amy White." She thrust out a hand. "And truly, if there's ever anything I can do… There's no way I can ever thank you."

A half-hour later, they were gone.

The house felt unbelievably empty.

Alex found the sudden stillness disquieting to the point of eerie. She sat in the middle of the bed, listening to the gurgle of the fountain.

She'd persuaded Amy to take their toys with her, but Amy assured her she already had not one, but two fountains at home. She still had all the litter boxes and food dishes.

And cat beds.

And cat palaces and condos for them to climb all over and in and out of.

Amy promised to email tons of pictures, and Alex trusted her at her word. Alex had more than just a knack about evaluating people and knew Amy wouldn't let her down.

Amy had even felt compelled to explain that Teyla hadn't been spayed yet because of an infection. She wanted to make sure Alex knew there wouldn't be any more litters.

Alex got up, determined to shake off the sadness. She could always go visit them.

The recollection of Teyla springing to the window, then leaping down to pounce joyously on her own mom had told Alex all she'd needed to know.

After nearly a whole year, Teyla—and her five little ones—were home where they belonged.

"Mysterious Angel" was previously published by Bluetrix Books in 2019 in The Angel Cat Collection *and is also available for sale as a single.*

Percy & Chauvelin

SKITTY: SEPTEMBER 2016
Amber Davis

ONE EARLY SEPTEMBER MORNING I DRIVE TO MY DAUGHTER'S PRESCHOOL. She's ready to go, bows in her hair, backpack on her back. I park on a small street called Tabor next to a busy Cottman Avenue in Philadelphia. Upon parking, I spot a small calico cat on the top of someone's sloped lawn. I called to her and did *pspspsp* but she never looked my way. I took my daughter to her new classroom, and after tearful goodbyes, I went back to my car to find the cat was gone. I shrugged it off, thinking they let their cat out, much to my disapproval because of a busy street like Cottman Avenue and the dangers of cars and strangers.

Over the months, I spot this little cat on and off, on the lawn or the steps of this home and she is always just laying, chilling, relaxing. Looking a bit skinny and disheveled, but I never dare approach as this cat is on someone's property and close to a busy road. One rainy day, I did however see her at the bottom of the steps, wet, just sitting, seemingly in a daze of thought. I approached her and she didn't seem to hear me coming. I reached out to pet her and she jumped, startled, and ran up the lawn and disappeared to the yard of the house. I decided to leave a note for the homeowners asking if cat was theirs, if they needed food, vetting, etc. as the cat was very skinny and looked a bit beaten up. I waited a few weeks with no phone call or email, but continued to see this cat.

Cue December, we are due to get a huge snowstorm later that afternoon, promising fifteen to twenty inches of snow with temperatures in the teens for a few days. Remembering this cat, my heart breaks, and I made a promise to myself, if this cat was there today, I would take her and leave a note. I pull up with my daughter in tow, and sure enough, she's a small ball up on the sloped frozen lawn. I take my daughter to her classroom, and come back out. I did not bring a carrier, as I was hoping she would be inside. I put on my gloves and heaved up the sloped grass, snuck behind this cat, and scruffed her, supporting her bottom with my free hand. The cat froze in fear and allowed me to scoop it up and put in my car. She sat curled up on the floor in the rear, on her best behavior, not making a peep of protest, enjoying the heat of the car. I hastily wrote a note and put it in their mailbox and headed home.

I unloaded this cat into my art studio and gave her food, water, and a heating pad to warm up. Upon further inspection, this cat was bone thin, scarred up, flea-infested, and made "tic-tac" noses when she walked on the hardwood floor. Later that day when my husband came home, he helped me look her over to find her nails were completely overgrown and curled into her pads, making walking incredibly painful for her. We took her to the vet to find she was anemic, in early stages of kidney failure, deaf, toothless, and weighed only 4 lbs. They estimated her to be around 15 years old. We decided to keep her in that room (away from my resident cats and my daughter) to keep her warm, safe, happy, and content until we heard from her owners.

About a week later, I get a phone call from the homeowners where this cat was found. They were an elderly couple who informed me the neighbors a few doors down were evicted about twelve years ago and left the cat behind. With the wife being overly allergic, they could not bring the cat inside, so they always fed her dry food and kept a dog house for her out back of their home. They were very happy and thankful to hear I took her in for vet care and the treatment she needed.

We did manage to trim her overgrown curled nails, much to her displeasure. It seemed she needed to learn to work properly again afterward as she was very painful and stiff. Though she was deaf, she did startle easy and was grouchy sometimes and was not a fan of other cats and small children. However, she absolutely loved eating her dry and wet food; her lack of teeth did not stop her from eating her fill. Her favorite spot was in the soft cat bed under the window where the sun shone in all day. Her meows were always super loud and purrs were soft but she was happy and content, until about five months later and her small frail body could take no more.

My husband returned from the vet with her pawprint on a cement stone and I wrote a tearful note and included photos to leave at the doorstep of the home where she lived outdoors all her life. She had a

Skitty

long rough life outdoors, but knew warmth, love, and a full belly for the remainder of her days.

If you move, please don't leave your cat behind, outside. They were fed and loved all the life they knew and do NOT know how to "live outdoors like wild cats" Most cats are not as lucky as Skitty, to have kind people looking after her.

CARETAKERS
Will McDermott

**To: Agent F. Mulder, FBI Headquarters, Washington, D.C.
FROM: Ms. Alex Betts, Roseville, California**

Dear Agent Mulder,

First off, I need you to know that I am not crazy. I do know you are a fictional character from an ancient television show and that there is no X-Files division at the FBI.

That being said, I certainly hope there is someone there who actually investigates weird, paranormal cases. I mean, someone put together that report on UFOs a few years back!

So, I'm hoping that addressing this package to you will get it into the hands of the real-life agents assigned to the real-life X-Files division. You understand, don't you? I need you to be real because the shit I am about to tell you is very real.

You may not recognize my name, but I was briefly famous last year when I rescued a lost cat that had somehow traveled all the way from Yellowstone National Park in Wyoming to my town of Roseville, California. That's eight hundred miles! Amazing, right?

Maybe I should have suspected something was strange about that cat at the time, but it seemed so normal, and it was half-dead, so I just wanted to protect it. But that's exactly what it wanted me to think.

I'm getting ahead of myself. Let me tell you how I found the tiny booklet included with this letter and then you can decide for yourself if something about all of this is weird. When you read it, you'll know I'm not crazy.

After I took Rayne Beau... That's the cat's human-given name; you'll see he calls himself by another name. After the Placir SPCA reunited Rayne Beau with the Anguianos family in Salinas, I went back to the green space across from my office where I originally found him. I heard he had lost his collar and hoped to be able to return it to Benny and Susanne Anguianos.

Well, I found the collar inside the same culvert Rayne Beau had crawled out of. It was covered in blood. But that wasn't the weird part. Hanging from the collar was a bulging pendant with a bent hinge. I forced it open, thinking there would be photos of the Anguianos couple and Rayne Beau inside.

But when it popped open, I found the tiniest little booklet I've ever seen. The whole thing was bulging from being wet, so I had to dry it out completely before looking inside.

I wish I'd never opened that booklet. I wish I hadn't read it. In fact, I wish I had left the whole thing alone. My life would be so much better right now if I had never gone into that roadside ditch green space in the first place when I heard Rayne Beau — that so-called cat — mewing.

I don't know what to do now. I can't sleep. I'm scared for my life. I'm scared for the lives of the Anguianos family. So, I've sent the booklet to you. Read it and you'll know I'm not crazy. Maybe you can do something about what happens next. I'm washing my hands of the whole thing. I need to regain control over my life. I may even move.

Yours in fear,

Alex Betts

Mission Log — June 5, 2024

Caretaker Akicitas reporting. I am on my way to the place the New Humans call Yellowstone — what the Ancient Tribes called the Burning Mountains. The tribes knew better than to travel through those scalding, hot lands. They knew the dangers. Modern humans never believe anything can harm them. That's why we Caretakers must stay vigilant.

I would have started earlier, but my current host family have been somewhat difficult to train. After I got the call about the situation with Caretaker Akiassee, it took some time to convince Benny and Susanne they needed to go on a thousand-mile camping trip.

We should arrive tomorrow and then I will begin my hunt. I hope Akiassee fully recovers. We've worked together several times, including when we quelled the Old One uprising that caused so much damage around the Great Western Bay a century back.

Mission Log — June 7, 2024

We entered the Burning Mountains today. After giving Susanne the slip, I made my way toward the spot where Akiassee was ambushed and picked up the scent of my prey. But something was off. It was definitely wendigo. Their stench is unmistakable. But there seemed to be a lot of them. I could barely breathe from the overpowering acrid taste in the back of my mouth and nose.

Perhaps an entire family had been turned, but in all my years, I'd never seen more than two wendigo banded together. Of course, I'd heard the tales of what happened in the area the New Humans call Donner Pass, but I don't know how that disaster could happen today. Still, my nose doesn't lie. There were at least a half-dozen monsters, maybe more.

Plus, there was something else. I caught just a whiff of a different scent that was almost completely masked by the foul odor of decay and rotting flesh. Something much older. I'm not certain what. But if I'm right—if something more dangerous is working with the wendigo—it might explain how a warrior of Akiassee's stature could have been ambushed.

I followed the pungent trail to an abandoned ranger cabin deep in the woods. I knew Susanne would worry if I didn't return before morning, but she would wait for me. I trained her and Benny that well, at least.

Besides, something about the cabin was gnawing at my hind leg as well. I wasn't sure what it was, but I dared not leave until I figured out the double mystery of the cabin and the odd odor. So, I decided to stake out the cabin to see what transpired. The last thing I wanted was to make the same mistake as Akiassee and rush in without all the information.

Mission Log — June 10, 2024

Scat! My impatience nearly cost me a life today. I fared better than Akiassee, but the mission is far from over. Here's what happened.

The wendigo family returned to the cabin late last night with their latest kill—some poor hiker who must have wandered too far off the trails. The hiker was already half-eaten when they returned, so I decided to watch for the extra scent to show up and also wait for the wendigo to sleep off their feast.

A couple hours before sunrise, no other monsters had appeared. I didn't want to risk any early risers, so I slipped into the cabin through a broken window and padded over to the closest wendigo.

Its leathery skin was drawn so tightly against its ribs, hips, and limbs that it looked almost skeletal. Wendigo eat and eat and eat but remain ravenous. That's what makes them so dangerous. But that was about to change.

I extended my claws and raked them swift and hard across the exposed neck of the closest monster. It barely gurgled as its last breath escaped through the long slits in its throat.

One down, six to go.

I made my way methodically around the cabin, slicing and dicing wendigo throats into shredded ribbons of meat, cartilage, and bone.

I had just two left, but when I reached the penultimate wendigo, that other scent, something foul and ancient, wafted off the corpse-like body. I admit it. I hesitated. And that almost cost me a life.

Before I could rake my claws through this monster's neck, its eyes fluttered open. Big, yellow, canine eyes! It was a scatting skin-walker wearing the skin of a wendigo.

My claws slashed down toward its exposed neck, but the skin-walker was too fast. It grabbed me by the collar and flung me across the room before jumping to its feet.

I landed on my feet, of course, and prepared to leap back into the fray. I couldn't kill it without learning its true name, but I could make it wish it were dead—for Akiassee's sake—while containing it until reinforcements arrived.

But the skin-walker was smarter than I gave him credit for. I realized my paws were ice-cold. I had landed on the chest of the last wendigo.

Their cannibalistic hearts truly are made of ice. Its chest was actually frosted over, forcing me to extend my claws to leap back into the fray. But, when the razor-like tips dug into the monster's leathery skin, it awoke with a roar.

I tried to pounce back at the skin-walker, but the wendigo lashed out as I leapt and sent me sprawling across the floor. Before I could turn around, the ice-hearted monster was on me again. They move fast for starving, half-frozen cannibals.

I had precious little time to deal with the last wendigo. If the skin-walker caught me again, it would be nothing for it to rip me in twain in its powerful, wolf jowls. Which I'm sure is what happened to Akiassee.

So, I dashed up the wendigo's bony legs and sliced my claws right through its groin, twice, back and forth. This made the beast double over around me, protecting me for the moment from the skin-walker and bringing its fleshy neck into range of my claws.

With one more slice, the last wendigo crumpled to the dusty floor, as dead as its brothers and sisters. But, for the moment, I lay trapped beneath it, caught in the leathery folds of its limbs and torso.

By the time I clawed my way out to freedom, the skin-walker had disappeared.

Mission Log — June 13, 2024

I tracked the skin-walker back to the campground where I had left Benny and Susanne. For a moment, I feared for their lives, although the skin-walker had no reason to target them specifically. Luckily, they were up early and away from the camper. Apparently, they were off searching for me. I could hear Benny rustling through the woods calling my name.

I wanted to go to them. Let them know I was okay. They're good humans, and I didn't want them to suffer because of me. But that's exactly why I needed to stay on the trail of the walker. He would kill again, and once he did, he would take a new skin, and I might lose him.

I couldn't let that happen.

I turned away from Benny's calls and prowled through the campground, following the beast's pungent odor. I didn't find the walker, but the scent lead me to his wendigo skin, abandoned in the bushes near the showers, next to the skinless remains of a woman who's only mistake this morning had been wanting a shower while the skin-walker sought a new skin.

I felt like I'd coughed up a furball. My mistakes had cost some poor human their life.

I moved away from the acrid smell of the dead wendigo skin and skinless dead human to search for the skin-walker scent again. It took me a while, but I finally found the scent, which had been heavily masked by soapy shower water and less-soapy bathroom fumes.

Why humans are willing to bathe where they defecate is beyond me, but at least I had the trail again, which led toward the campers at the far end of the camp. As I began padding in that direction, I heard a camper engine roar to life.

I reached the edge of the campground in time to see a Winnebago tear around the edge of the lot toward the exit. The driver, a woman who's skin looked ill-fitting glared back at me. Her yellow eyes shone briefly in the fluorescent lights at the edge of the access road.

I tore through the forest toward the main road to get ahead of the big, slow camper. I had to see which way it turned. I got there just in time to see it head southwest. Not much to go on, but I had to try.

I looped back to the campground. Benny and Susanne were deep in the forest searching for me, so that was going to take too long. Luckily, I saw a family packing up. I hopped in the back of their SUV and began meowing like my life was in peril. Which was only half a lie.

It felt like I spent an interminable amount of time convincing these people to both hurry up and to take me with them. But in reality, it probably took less than fifteen minutes. They had obviously been very well trained by a previous cat-master.

Soon, we were tooling down the highway, heading west. I convinced them to open the window so I could track the skin-walker. Any other beast I would have lost, but its strong scent carried on the wind for miles, which was lucky because it turned onto a highway heading almost due south within just a few miles.

At least we were heading in the right direction. Every time this nice family tried to turn away from the skin-walker's scent, I caterwauled loud and long until they changed their minds.

I'm sure they thought they were returning me to my home. Little did I know that this ruse would become too true for me all too soon.

Mission Log — June 18, 2024

After days of forcing my temporary family to drive almost due south through Wyoming and Utah, we entered Nevada and began heading west again. Then, yesterday morning, I forced them to turn into the parking lot of the Overland Hotel and Saloon in Pioche, Nevada, where the skin-walker's trail ended.

I don't know why the skin-walker brought its new family here. Perhaps it just needed a rest or had figured out I was on its trail and wanted to change bodies and cars again. But it seemed like a gigantic coincidence that it chose this hotel of all places. You see, I have some history here.

The current Caretakers Council members may not remember, but I was sent here more than 200 years ago to handle a "ghost" problem. Just like this little "wendigo" job, the Overland Hotel ghost turned out to be anything but a ghost. I had to employ an actual catholic priest to exorcise that damned demon.

But I digress.

Whatever the reason, the skin-walker had brought me back to the Overland. It turned out it even booked Room 10, the very spot where the exorcism took place. But, again, it all could be a coincidence. The hotel went to great lengths to play up the "Ghost Story" of Room 10. It was in all the brochures. Of course, they got every fact wrong and didn't even mention me.

But he was here, and I needed to stop him before he killed again. So, as soon as we stopped, I leapt through the open window of the SUV and ran straight into the hotel lobby and began cuddling up against the desk manager, a young woman by the name of Adele who, coincidentally, was the great-great-granddaughter of the woman who ran the place back when I saved the day, no thanks from any of the humans, as usual.

When my temporary family rushed in and found me seemingly at home, they asked the manager if I was her cat. I cuddled hard against her face and mouth before she could answer. She shrugged at them and said, "Sure looks like it."

And that was that. I had freed my transportation to get on with their lives. I hoped they decided to head back out immediately, but they decided to stay the night.

I needed to get that skin-walker before he got to them.

Late last night, I slipped into Room 10 to deal with the walker once and for all. The room looked almost identical to how it had 200 years earlier, except with a lot less blood on the walls. The stench of the beast I was after filled the room and my nostrils.

It was everywhere.

I checked the two cots before moving to the main bed. Each had a young child fast asleep, but reeking of skin-walker. I began to get a very bad feeling about this situation. I made my way to the four-poster bed. Atop the thick mattress lay the father, who also reeked of skin-walker.

But none of them had been replaced. The monster had simply covered them in its pheromones to throw me off. The mother of the family, the woman who's bloody carcass I had found near the wendigo skin in Yellowstone, was nowhere to be seen.

I dashed from the room and down the hall to the room where my temporary family were sleeping. But there was no walker stench emanating from that room. I slipped inside just to be sure, and I could see them all asleep by the light of the nearly full moon streaming through the window.

The full moon. Like werewolves, the skin-walkers' distant, European cousins, these new-world shapeshifters drew power from the moon and were never more dangerous than under the influence of the light of a full moon. And it's not just the one day, either. Most books get that wrong. Shape-shifter attacks peak on the day of the full moon, but the two days leading up to it and after it are just as dangerous.

I had to find the walker fast. But where had it gone? If it was still intent on evading me, I thought it might grab the skin of a horse. It had been a wendigo, so why not another mindless beast? That would give it speed and the ability to avoid roads, which would slow me down.

I jumped onto the windowsill to look down on the stables behind the hotel. Sure enough, I saw the yellow-eyed woman sneaking toward the barn doors. But I also saw a light on inside the stable! Someone was in there, and I was fairly certain I knew who.

I jumped from the window and landed on my feet on the ground fifteen feet below. I raced toward the stable but heard the screams as I crossed the distance.

The stable doors were slightly ajar, so I ran for the crack between them. I planned to rush in and confront the shapeshifter as it worked to don its victim's skin.

But I underestimated the speed the moon's power gave it. Before I reached the doors, they slammed open and great-great-granddaughter Adele, eyes flashing yellow, rode through the widening doors atop a great stallion. She disappeared into the night, once again heading west.

Mission Log — June 21, 2024

After losing the skin-walker in Pioche, I hopped a train to Carson City. I had a pretty good idea where the beast in granddaughter's clothing was going next, so I wanted to get ahead of him for once.

I'm not sure why, but this skin-walker seems to have a grudge against me. I finally figured it out when I realized why that abandoned cabin in Yellowstone made my hind leg itch. Caretaker Akiassee and I had worked another case together that led to that very cabin. So, the Akiassee attack and use of the abandoned ranger cabin where the two of us had banished a swarm of mosquito men was just to lure me out.

Then, the next place the walker stopped was the Overland Hotel. And of all the people he could choose for a new skin, he just happened to grab the great-great-granddaughter of one of my former human pets.

The bastard was targeting all my greatest wins and trying to turn them into losses. I didn't know why, but it didn't matter because I had him. The walker was headed for the Clown Hotel in Tonopah, Nevada. I won't describe what happened there. If you want to know, look up the sanitized version in the annals. That place still haunts me, and I won't discuss it.

But I wasn't going to Tonopah. At least not yet. First, I had to visit an old friend in Carson City. I didn't know this skin-walker's true name, so I needed a medicine man who could create a sacred weapon.

Luckily, I knew a guy. Well, the grandson of a guy, but he went into the family business.

As soon as I walked into Setting Son's shop, I could feel the power of the place. The kid, now pushing eighty himself, looked up at me and flashed a huge, wide grin that nearly cracked his ancient, brown skin.

Turns out, Son had been waiting for me. He'd heard about the strange happenings across Wyoming and Nevada and just knew I had to be in the middle of it all.

I leapt onto the counter and sidled up against Son. I'd forgotten how much I missed a little human contact. I told him I was tracking a skin-walker who seemed to know a lot about me, so I needed an edge—the edge of a sacred weapon to be exact.

He had just the thing.

Son reached beneath the counter and pulled out a short, curved blade with a leather-wrapped, bone handle. Red and black ribbons trailed from the guard, representing power and death respectively. The ribbons had been tied on with what I could tell was cord made from the intestines of a bison for a little extra *oomph*.

I didn't ask where he'd gotten that particular, very illegal, ingredient as he handed me the blade. Good thing, too. Son had more than just the blade for me. He had intel on the skin-walker I'd been trailing.

Son told me the walker had already blown through Tonopah two days earlier, where he'd taken the current owner of the Clown Hotel, before heading toward Carson City. Once in Carson City, the walker didn't waste any time in his clown skin.

He apparently grabbed some kid right out from under the noses of her parents while they toured Bliss Mansion during a "Ghost Walk."

That tracked. I worked the Bliss Mansion haunting way back in the Wild West days. Scatting railroad baron built his house atop an actual tribal burial site. Son's grampa and I had to put all those poor souls to rest before they took out the whole town.

I asked Son where I could find this kid as I twirled the sacred blade between my claws. After admonishing me about talking about a kid like that while twirling a blade, Son gave me the bad news.

The walker's new family had already left Carson City on their way to Reno. But he said that after Reno, the parents were heading to Roseville, California.

That tracked. I had business in Roseville a couple decades ago. Nothing in Reno, though, so maybe that side trip wasn't part of the skin-walker's revenge plot.

Better yet, Son had arranged quick transportation for me to Roseville. Now, Setting Son knows I hate planes, especially small ones with open seating, so I was not at all surprised to find that his "quick transport" was a single-engine crop duster owned by a friend of his.

But to his credit, Son gave me one last bit of information he'd discovered about the skin-walker before I took off for Roseville. Apparently, I knew this walker's sire. In fact, Akiassee and I had killed his sire about fifty years ago. Son didn't know the walker's name, though, but now that I had the sacred weapon, I didn't need the bastard's name.

Mission Log — June 24, 2024

Well, everything went according to plan… until it didn't.

The address Son had given me for the family whose daughter the walker had replaced was accurate and I arrived before they got home from Reno.

Several hours after the lights went out inside, I slipped through an open window and followed the ancient stench of the skin-walker straight to the girl's room. I even checked the parents' room first to make sure the scatting walker didn't fool me again by spreading his scent around the family.

Everyone was asleep, so I padded back to the girl's room, where the stench was the strongest. She lay there asleep in the dark, reeking of decaying skin. I had him. Finally. It seemed certain I would finish this hunt right then and there.

I padded into the girl's room, leapt silently onto the foot of her bed, and prowled up toward her head—and her exposed neck, the sacred blade clenched between my teeth.

I grabbed the blade from my mouth, raised it over her slender neck, and mewed the proper prayers to summon the sacred spirits to aid me in dispatching this abomination of evil.

That's when the lights flared to life overhead, the mother shrieked behind me, and everything went to scat.

The walker's yellow eyes, too big for the little girl's cherubic face, flashed open beneath my blade as I tried to plunge the tip into the tender flesh of his throat.

The mother shrieked again and rushed forward. The walker raised its spindly, child arms to fend me off, but only managed to divert the blade to the side. It bit flesh but missed the carotid.

The mother slammed into me before I could pull the blade free to try again, sending us both tumbling off the bed. I landed atop her chest and pounced back up onto the bed, hoping to finish the job before anything else went wrong. The mother might send me off to a shelter afterward, where I would be put down for killing her baby, but at least the job would be done.

Except, of course, I no longer had the blade. He did.

As soon as I landed on the bed, I saw the blade flash toward me. The walker had no strength in those spindly, little-girl arms, but he still had the speed and experience of a monster to guide it home.

The sacred blade plunged into my abdomen as I tried to twist and leap out of the way. Blood streamed from the wound and matted my fur. The walker raised the blade again, the blood spilling from his own neck wound running down his slim arms to wet the blade.

Behind me the mother had risen and screamed bloody murder at me. Caught between protective parent and knife-wielding child monster, I had no choice but to flee. I leapt at the mother's face, forcing her to duck and raced through the house for the open window where I had entered.

Mission Log — July 29, 2024

It's been a month since the bedroom debacle. I haven't had the time or strength to complete a report in that time. Since the walker stabbed me, I've been on the run. I patched the wound the best I could, but I lost a lot of blood — and that was before the wound got infected.

On top of that, the walker has been hunting me. First it came for me in the body of the mother. I'm sure she was taken soon after she witnessed her own daughter nearly fatally stabbing a demon cat. Poor woman. She didn't ask for that. None of them did.

I don't care a hairball for my life at this point. I failed the humans of Roseville and everyone between here and Yellowstone. He's taken so many in the relentless pursuit of his petty revenge. I should just let him take me and be done with it. But I know the killing won't stop there.

I need to find some way to get this report to the Council, so they can send another Caretaker to finish the job I failed. But I can feel him closing in. Even if there were another Caretaker in Roseville, I couldn't get my logbook to them before he catches up to me.

I need help. I'm sure he'll find me here in this drainpipe any day now…

Ring-ring. Ring-ring.
"Hello?"
"Is this Ms. Betts? Ms. Alex Betts?"
"Who's calling?"
"You can call me Mulder. Agent in Charge Mulder. I'm with the FBI Extraordinary Cases Unit. And no, that is not my real name, but I think you know why I am calling."
"You got my package."
"Yes, ma'am. I have agents on their way right now to the Anguianos residence in Salinas, but I have a few questions."
"I was sure you all were going to think I was crazy."
[Silence]
"Yes, ma'am. We get that a lot. Can you tell me where the rest of the booklet is? The reports you sent us were incomplete."

"That was all I found. That's why I was so concerned. As far as I know, Rayne Beau, or Akicitas as he calls himself, never made another mission log. I think that creature must have found him and killed him. I think the skin-walker(?) took Rayne Beau's skin and tricked me into returning him to the Anguianos's home so he could complete his revenge."

"Not possible, ma'am. Rayne Beau was identified by his microchip, which is placed subdermally, meaning it's implanted beneath the skin."

"I know what it means! But what about all that blood on his collar? Where did that come from?"

[Silence]

"Hello? Agent Mulder? Hello?"

"Just a routine check-in, right?" Agent Hayes asked as they exited the sedan. The sun was shining, and the street was calm and almost too suburban for Hayes's liking. It was the place white people went to die long, lonely deaths. He'd never be caught dead living here.

"Yeah," replied Special Agent Matthews. The AIC thinks there's nothing here. We just need to follow up to be certain."

As they walked toward the front door, Matthews hesitated beside Hayes and then reached into his inside jacket pocket to grab his phone, which was buzzing.

"Speak of the AIC," he said, waving the phone in the air. "Go ring the doorbell while I see what he wants."

Hayes gave his senior partner a quick thumbs-up, but he already knew what their boss wanted. The man had only recently been promoted and had not yet learned the fine art of managing without micromanaging.

Hayes didn't give the matter another thought as he rapped his brown knuckles on the red door set into the white front porch. *What was it with white people and their red doors?* He wondered as he heard an old person shuffling toward the door inside. *Not enough color in their lives?*

The door opened and Hayes nodded at the short, plump Mrs. Anguianos. Almost white, gray hair surrounded her face in a style she'd probably worn since watching *Friends* in college.

"Mrs. Anguianos?" Hayes inquired. "I'm Agent Hayes with the FBI. May I and my partner come in for a few minutes?"

Hayes motioned back to Matthews, who seemed a bit animated for someone just providing a check-in to an overbearing boss.

"What is this about?" Mrs. Anguianos asked. "We're not in some sort of trouble, are we?"

She glanced over her shoulder and cried out, "Benny! The FBI is here. Did you and your drinking buddies break that pinball machine again?"

"Hayes!" Matthews yelled behind him. "Hayes! Step away from the door. Right now!"

Hayes glanced back at his partner, who had brandished his weapon and was pointing it at the door. Dumbfounded, Hayes turned back to Mrs. Anguianos.

He saw just the briefest flash of yellow eyes before the short, plump, old woman grabbed him by the arm and yanked him off his feet with surprising ease.

Hayes went sprawling across the hardwood floor inside the foyer as the skin-walker slammed the door behind him. He tried to roll over and grab his own weapon, but the spry, old lady was on top of him before he could move a muscle.

Shots rang out and splinters flew as Matthews fired several shots through the door. But Hayes had read the mission briefing. If Mrs. Anguianos was indeed the skin-walker that had terrorized the western states these past couple months, neither he nor Matthews had any chance against it. At least not without its true name.

As Mrs. Anguianos ripped at his back and the nape of his neck, the door flew open behind Hayes. He braced himself for Matthews to unload his weapon into the monster atop him.

Instead, he heard the yowl of a cat, which made Mrs. Anguianos pause. She leapt off his back, giving Hayes a chance to roll over and scramble back against the wall.

There he was. Rayne Beau, his fur dirty and short, but not bloody, except for a small wound just visible between his shoulder blades as he stalked around the deadly walker.

"Thought I was dead, didn't you!" Rayne Beau hissed as the two beasts circled one another like two cage fighters looking for an opening. "Left me there, deep in that drainpipe, soaked in my own blood."

"You were dead!" the walker screamed back. "I took your skin. I took your chip. Your body was cold!"

"Turns out I still have one or two lives left," Rayne Beau replied. "Unlike you, Ragamore, son of Morerag. Your father should have been better at names, if you ask me."

The skin-walker gasped at the utterance of his name. And at that, Rayne Beau pointed a set of claws at Hayes. "Now, if you please!"

But Hayes was too slow on the uptake. To be fair, he would tell Matthews later, he'd just been attacked by a monster, which Matthews then reminded him was just a little old lady."

Instead, Matthews stormed through the door behind the Caretaker cat and opened fire. He put five bullets into the chest of the monstrous old lady in a tight grouping. She dropped to the floor, a very surprised look in her yellow eyes, before sliding out of Mrs. Anguianos's skin.

Even faced with that horror show, Hayes only had one question on his mind.

"You can talk?" he gasped at Rayne Beau. "Can all cats talk?"

"Yes," the cat replied. "We just choose not to."

Ring-ring. Ring-ring.

"Hello, Agent Mulder."

"That's Agent in charge… you know what? Never mind. Thank you for all your help, Ms. Betts."

"Is it over, then?"

"Yes."

"Thank god. I haven't slept in so long. Any word on Caretaker Akicitas? That poor thing."

"In fact, yes. You'll be seeing him quite soon."

"That's great… Wait! What do you mean by that?"

"A little reward for your assistance in this difficult case. Besides, Rayne Beau needs a new home."

"I never agreed to this–"

Click.

Ding-dong!

Reprinted with permission from Castle of Horror #12 ©2025 Castle Bridge Media.

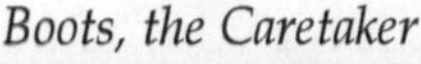

Boots, the Caretaker

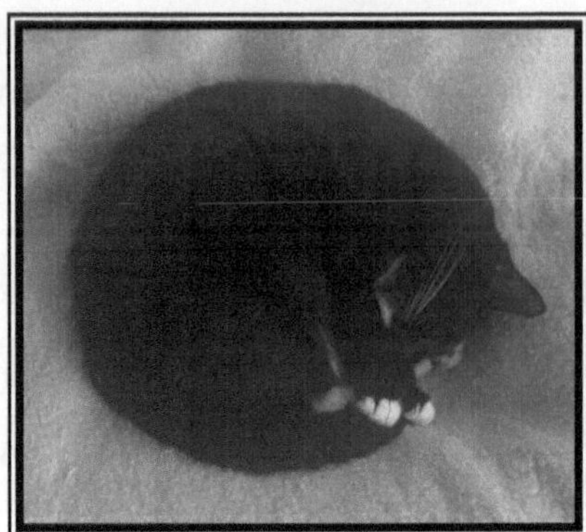

3 AM
Jacob Jones-Goldstein

THE HOUSE IS DARK AND QUIET LATE AT NIGHT. I'M CURLED UP IN A cardboard box. It's a good box, although it's getting close to the end of its use. I like to move around and sleep in different places. Being predictable leads to complacency, and complacency is deadly when *they* come.

I never sleep that deeply this time of night. My people have been in bed for hours by now, and from the sounds coming from the room they are slumbering. It's not hard to tell with the fat one. He makes more noise sleeping than he does when he's awake. It's harder to tell with the woman. She makes noises, but they're different, and she talks a lot. They don't sound like her regular words. They're low and mumbly, more like noises than the words she says when she's awake.

The other cat, Noodle, is in there with them. I'd like to say they were protected with her in there, but I cannot. She's a waste. A big trundling mess of a thing. We tolerate each other, but she knows that I'm in charge of the place, even if she'll never admit it. She pretends she is because she sleeps on the bed. I could sleep on the bed if I wanted to, but I must remain vigilant.

It's early yet, but I'm awake, so I decided to do a quick reconnaissance. I pad down the darkened hallway to the bedroom. Everything seems in order. As I hop up onto the chest at the end of the bed to survey the landscape, Noodle wakes up and glares at me. I glare back. She is curled up between them, and even has her head on one of the pillows like some kind of queen. I roll my eyes at her. She lays her head back down and burbles for a moment before dozing off again.

Noodle came from a shelter about a year after I arrived here. I don't understand why she's such a soft ball of fur and laziness. Sure, she'll take a swipe at me once in a while, but most of the time, when I initiate training, she just yowls and gets me sprayed with the water from the bottle. Ours is an uneasy truce. Shelter cats should be harder than that. She should be ready for anything, certainly ready for when *they* come at night, but instead, she lounges around and sleeps on the bed. I'm not sure she even knows *they* exist.

I hop down from the chest and check the closet. Nothing out of the ordinary. As I double back and return to the box, I hear the woman stir. Her soft murmuring stops and doesn't restart. Eventually, she stands up and walks toward me. Slinking back into the shadows, I let her pass unmolested. She stumbles to the bathroom and, after a while, comes back. I like to think she knows that I have her protected, but I'm not sure she understands. To be honest, when *they* show up, she is more of a hindrance than a help. Humans are like that.

Once I think she is asleep, I walk back down the hall and do a check of the other rooms. Everything is quiet. Feeling satisfied, I head back to the box and curl up. I think this will be the last night in this box. Complacency.

As I sleep, I dream of my younger days in my other home. The man in that home was not kind. He fed me and gave me shelter, but it was only begrudgingly. When I was very young, I tried to be like Noodle. I would get on the bed with him or sit on the couch with him. Always he would rebuff my attempts at friendship. It was a lonely way to be for both of us, but it also steeled me to my duty. I was here to protect, not to cuddle or comfort. It was there I learned to stay vigilant, not only for *them* but for him. His moods were unpredictable, and often, it was best to seek out-of-the-way places when he was angry.

It was the first night *they* came that ended our relationship. A light was destroyed in the chaos that I was blamed for. He put me out and closed the door. When the woman I live with now found me and forced me to suffer the indignity of being picked up, as she brought me back, he closed the door on me again. I have been in this home ever since.

In my dreams, I am back there, cowering from his anger. It is not a good dream. When I wake I feel on edge, shaken. I know that I do not need to fear my people in the same way now, but those memories do not die quietly.

The night is still. The noise from the other room has quieted down. All of them must be in deeper sleep. I stretch and shift before I return to my slumber. Perhaps *they* will not come tonight.

Time passes in the dark quiet of the night until I hear a noise. I slowly open one eye but do not move. Surveying around me I don't see anything. I quiet my breathing and listen. The normal night noises filter through. It's possible that I was dreaming. I wait for a while but eventually begin to drift off to sleep. That is when I hear it again.

Immediately, I am up and running toward the noise. It came from the room where the woman and the fat one eat their meals. I run down the hall through the kitchen, achieving top speed just as I make the turn into the eating room. The floors are made of wood, much to my chagrin, and I lose my grip during the turn and go sliding across the room and into the wall. I bounce off the wall and leap onto the table to grab the higher ground. Unfortunately, the people have put the cloth on the table again and I failed to notice. It provides no purchase as both the cloth and I slide off the table, landing in a heap on the floor.

As I struggle to extricate myself, I hear the noise again. This time, it's from the room I was in. *They* may have tried to lure me away. Wasting no time, I tear back through the kitchen, or at least I try to. The cloth is still wrapped around me, slowing me down. Eventually, it falls away, and I enter the room at top speed, leaping at the last moment and landing in my box. If *they* were lurking here waiting for me, they will be in for a surprise.

They were not. I land going faster than I had planned, and it sends the box, with me in it, tumbling into a bookshelf. Something falls from the top and hits the carpet with a muffled thump. *They* might be dropping things on me. Fearing attack, I hop sideways away from the bookcase and jump onto the top of the couch. I flatten myself and dig my claws in to make sure I have solid purchase. Panting slightly, I survey the room. Everything seems to be in order.

Near the box is the thing that fell from the shelf. It is one of the small plastic things shaped like people. It could be one of *them* in disguise.

Deciding to investigate, I hop down and approach it cautiously. From a slight distance, I sniff it. It smells normal. Reaching out my paw I tentatively bat it. It doesn't move. To be safe, I bat it around a few times. It rolls away from me slightly, so I pounce on it. It never moves on its own. I feel satisfied that it is just a plastic thing and smack it one last time so that it rolls under the couch. Best to not have obstacles lying around in the open if things get serious.

Another sound.

This time from the hall closet.

If *they* are in there, then I will have them cornered. I bound back through the kitchen, jumping over the cloth, and this time slowing down to make the turn through the eating room. I still skid across the floor, but not so far this time. I am at full tilt again when I realize the closet door is closed. It's too late to completely slow down, so I turn to avoid going headfirst into the door but still hit it with a loud bang. I shake it off and go to work.

The door usually takes some time to open. It's hard to find purchase, so I begin scratching at it. This doesn't often work, but it is always worth trying. I rapidly run my claws across the surface. Nothing much happens, but if *they* are in there, then they'll know what they are facing.

I try to hook my claw on the edge and drag it open. It wiggles a little, just not enough. I try a few more times, but it doesn't budge. I yowl in frustration. I may not be able to get in, but they cannot get out. I resolve to stay vigilant and guard the door until the morning.

I stand by the door, a silent sentinel, for a few moments. I hear no more noises from inside. *They* must be cowering in fear. Unafraid of them, I begin to clean myself in a show of confidence.

Mid-lick, I hear another noise. This one isn't coming from the closet. It was from the bathroom. I don't hesitate before I am off down the hall once again.

I slow to a stop just outside. The door is mostly closed, but not all the way. I nudge it open a little with my head and begin to creep in. Nothing seems amiss, but the curtain is closed, hiding the tub beyond it.

I jump up on the sink to get a better vantage point and survey the area. Everything is still and quiet. They must be hiding behind the curtain. I have been silent as a shadow thus far, so *they* should not realize I am in here. I decide to trick them by making a noise of my own. Looking around there are plenty of things around the sink to use as decoys. I begin batting them over to the edge and then knocking them onto the floor one by one. After the third, I hear a noise but from outside the bathroom. *They* are trying to trick me. Immediately, I launch my attack. I dive from the sink onto the toilet and then into the hanging barrier with a primordial cry. It's heavier than expected and I don't get as far as I planned. Thinking fast, I extend my claws and grab hold of the vinyl. I dangle for a moment as it swings inward, and then I drop myself into the tub and into an inch of water.

I was not expecting the water. *They* must know how much I hate it. I scramble for purchase, but the water is below me, and the curtain is above me. Backing up is my only option to get out, and I do so as quickly as possible. My claws slip and scratch on the surface under the water, but eventually, I back up far enough to get free. Reaching the rear of the tub I brace myself for a second and then begin pumping my legs for momentum. I leap out of the tub, landing on the floor in a skid. The door is right there and I bash into it, shutting it. I yell in frustration, knowing *they* have fooled me.

The door hasn't latched, and I am able to wrap my paw around the edge enough to create space for my head. Once my head is in the opening, I am able to use it to throw the door open.

Soaking wet, I charge into the hall and down toward the living room. *They* won't be tricking me again. Barreling into the area, I surge to the top of the sofa and then onto the coffee table. I land on a pile of magazines, which softens my landing but doesn't slow me down. The magazines go flying off the table as I continue my charge. I will find *them*.

On through the kitchen and once again into the eating room. I don't see *them* anywhere, but I am determined. Back through the kitchen and into the living room again. From the living room, I glide into the foyer and into the den. *They* are still nowhere to be found. I rush back the way I came and once again vault on the couch.

From the top of the couch, I pause, panting. The house is silent. I wait a long while on my perch. There is no sound, not so much as a peep.

Eventually I hear a new kind of sound from the bedroom where my family sleeps. It is not the kind of noise *they* make but the kind the fat one makes when he is deep in his slumber.

I hop down from the couch, satisfied that *they* have retreated for the night. Tired but content that my work is done, I pad down the hall to let the people know.

They are both asleep when I arrive. Between his snoring and her ear plugs, they have once again slept through the invasion. Taking my spot on the chest at the foot of the bed, I let them know what I have done in a series of confident meows a few reassuring pats on their feet. They both stir and look up at me slightly. The fat one grumbles and rolls back over. The woman smiles and makes some comforting noises. As I stand there, she gets up and walks down the hall. I think she may be verifying my report.

Eventually, she comes back and, to my delight, gives me a reward. She drops several of the delicious treats in front of me before scratching the top of my head and climbing into bed.

I do what I do because it is what is expected of me, and I ask for no reward, but a few treats before sleeping is appreciated.

Since the box has been compromised, I will sleep here in the room with my family. There is a comfortable blanket on the chest that I curl up on. My belly is full from the treats, and I go to sleep with a sense of accomplishment.

In my dreams I am happy and was always here with them and never with the unkind man. They are good dreams.

Joby

Nelly

GINGER AND THE BULLY OF LOWERGATE COURT

Sharon Lee

FOR NINE YEARS STEVE AND I (WITH ARCHIE, ARWEN, BRANDEE, AND Buzz-z) lived in an impossible little townhouse on Lowergate Court in Owings Mills, Maryland. Lowergate was one of five courts that comprised the stunningly misnamed Bright Meadows, the entire campus of which was roughly three quarters of a mile around.

The best thing about Bright Meadows (besides that the rent was cheap and the roof kept the rain off. Mostly.) was that there were many dozens of cats in the neighborhood. Steve and I would go for walks up and down and around the various courts and say hi to Jazz and Mom, Sasquatch, Pirate, Taffy, Sandy, The Gentleman, Blue, and Ginger.

Ginger was the mayor. *I* didn't say he was the mayor — anyone could see that he was, just by looking at him. An orange striped cat of middle years with a habitual demeanor of grave attentiveness, he made his rounds every day, up, down, and around the courts, across to World's End and down the back woods.

He would stop by our place mid-morning and trade orange-cat stories with Archie through the bottom screen in the kitchen door. At least once I saw him at World's End with Brandee, hunting moles. He cuffed Buzz-z once when they first met and that took care of that — deference to the mayor was Buzz-z's rule, ever after.

Ginger was a non-partisan mayor. He was a cat, true enough, but he held every resident of the courts to be citizens, equally subject to his authority — and his protection. Steve saw him run off a stray dog that had frightened one of the toddlers in the playground. I saw him streaking to the rescue, the day Pirate was treed by a couple of boys with too much time on their hands.

The Gentleman, who was Brandee's special friend, was a Cat of the World — a wire-tough black-and-white with gnawed-up ears and a limp off the back right leg — and even he accorded Ginger the respect of his rank, whenever he found himself on Hizzoner's turf.

Not so, the Siamese.

I do not at this distance remember the Siamese's name. Perhaps I never knew it. Steve claims some vague recollection of having heard him called "Khan."

I'm not so sure. What I am sure of is that he arrived outside my kitchen door one April morning, just before Ginger's daily visit, swearing and cussing and hissing at Archie, who was standing up on his hind legs and giving back as good as he got. I threw a glass of water on him through the screen and told him to get a life, which, as it happens, was a mistake.

From that moment on, the Siamese targeted our house. He would show up at all hours, bitching and screaming. He would crouch under the bush by the door and leap on Brandee, or Steve or me as we left.

But we weren't the only ones.

He made Taffy's life a misery. He jumped The Gentleman so many times that The Gentlemen went to visit friends in the country. He clawed Jazz so badly the vet was afraid he wouldn't be able to save the eye. S'quatch would scream when he saw the Siamese coming his way and scramble up the drainpipe to sit wailing in the rain gutter until his lady fetched him down. Brandee would flatten herself to the ground and her ears to her head and dare him to try it, which was also Sandy's approach — damages there were minor, but the name-calling sessions were deafening.

Ginger tried to reason with him, to no avail. I tried to reason with his owner and was told to mind my own business and if that cat come missing, she'd know who to blame.

This went on from April until August.

And one hot August afternoon, with the heat beating out of the sky colliding with the heat rising off the tarmac at the level of your ears — up at the top of Lowergate Court, right next to the dumpster — an amazing thing occurred.

The Siamese was sitting in the parking lot, swearing at Pirate, who was scrunched down under a starveling cedar tree, pretending to be invisible.

They had been doing this for some time.

Suddenly, in other parts of the court, there was — movement.

From up-court came Mom and Sasquatch; from down-court, Brandee and Sandy. Taffy and Jazz drifted down the hill across and Blue pussyfooted in from somewhere and sat next to the cedar tree, tail wrapped around his toes.

The Siamese cut off in mid-curse and looked around him. The rest of the cats kept moving, slowly and purposefully, even Snowball-called-Avalanche, who never left her patio, until they had made a circle, with the Siamese in the center.

The Siamese yawned. He got up and headed for the gap between Jazz and Taffy. The cats moved closer together as he approached. Somebody growled. The Siamese backed up.

After a minute, he chose another direction, this one toward the cedar tree. He started to growl as he got closer and puffed himself up. But Pirate screamed back and made himself even bigger and Blue said something that was perhaps not quite polite.

The Siamese slunk back to the center of the circle and sat, carefully, down.

Which was when Ginger left his place in the ring and walked forward.

Immediately, the Siamese was on his feet, fur every-which-way, swearing like a ship full of sailors.

The circle of cats drew a little closer together. Ginger kept moving forward.

The Siamese flattened his belly to the tarmac and his ears to his head and swore he was the master of every cat there and a black belt in seventeen secret martial arts, besides.

Ginger kept coming.

The Siamese yelled for his mommy.

Ginger reached out and smacked him upside the head, none-too-gently. The Siamese babbled and wailed.

Ginger smacked him again, a little harder, but not nearly as hard as the Siamese had hit Jazz.

The Siamese stopped screaming. V-e-r-y slowly, he sat up. Even more slowly, he got his ears back into position. He licked his lips. Ginger sat down, utterly at ease, and began to bathe. All around, the cat circle waited.

They held that tableau for half-an-hour, I guess, then, one-by-one, the cats in the circle drifted away, back to their usual rounds. Ginger, spotlessly clean, left last, saving only the Siamese, who waited another four or five minutes, blue eyes darting this way and that. When he was certain he was unobserved, he got up and headed for home.

I never heard another ill word out of him, from that day until we moved.

First published in Central Maine Morning Sentinel, 1996.

Trooper

Archie

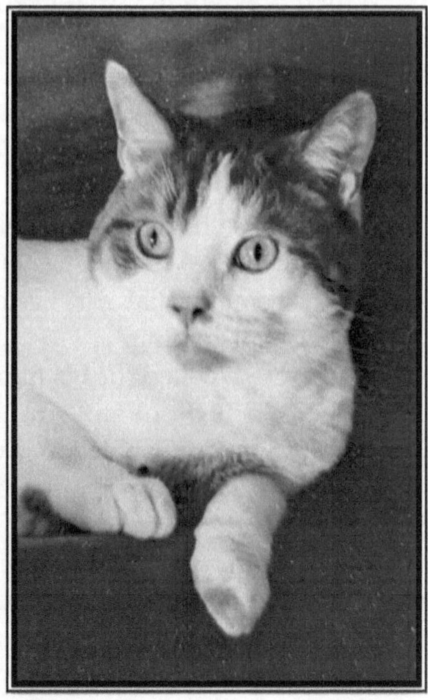

POOHBEAR & SMOKEY
Marc L Abbott

PRELUDE

THEY WERE SCHEDULE TO BE TERMINATED UNTIL GABRIEL KENNEDY AND his eight-year-old son, Simon, rescued them from the pound.

Gabriel Kenney didn't intend on adopting Poohbear and Smokey. Simon tearfully pleaded with him after hearing that animals who stayed in the pound too long were put to sleep.

"A dog and a cat? No, Simon, dogs and cats do not get along. They're natural enemies," Gabriel said.

"No, they're not. Alex in my class has a dog and a cat and they get along okay," his son said, his gaze earnest.

"He's right," the pound keeper said. "If they grow up together, they're going to get along. It's good to have one of each that way they don't feel lonely when you're off at work and school. And you're in luck because these two actually know one another."

"Dad, please, I promise I'll take real good care of them. They're puppy and kitten so it all works out and they're already friends."

Gabriel still wasn't moved. "That's because they let them mingle here."

"Actually, they knew one another before coming here."

"Really? What's their story?"

"They were abandoned by their previous owners after a foreclosure on the home. They were left behind. A lot of people do that when they can't afford to continue caring for their pets or can't take them with them to their new homes. Anyway, someone called animal rescue when they spotted the dog in the window a few days after the owners skipped town. He was barking up a storm. The cat, I was told, they found in one of the upper bedrooms refusing to leave the children's bedroom."

"That's sad," Gabriel said. "And no one has shown interest in them?"

"People have shown interest in them, but the thing is, they came in together and have a bond. We would prefer they got to a home together rather than split them up. That's the reason they're together in this cage."

Gabriel looked in the cage at the Husky/Chow mix dog then at the grey tabby. He watched as Simon knelt before the Husky. He placed his hand on the cage and the puppy licked his palm voraciously. The cat pawed while meowing loudly. Simon turned his attention to him.

"You're such a good kitty. Yeah, you're the best." He put a finger between the bars and scratched the cat's neck. The cat purred, welcoming the affection.

"Want me to let them out?" the keeper said.

"Yes!" Simon yelled.

"Simon, I don't think that's a good—"

Before he could finish the sentence, the keeper was at the cage and opened it. The puppy and tabby rushed out and swarmed all over Simon. He laughed and fell back on the floor as they showered him with affection.

The dog then turned to Gabriel. He barked and rushed to him.

"No-no-no!" he yelled. The puppy bounced on his hind legs, wagging his tail, begging to be picked up. Gabriel leaned down, started to pet his head, got licks on his hand and before he knew it, he had him in his arms. The puppy leaned up and licked his face, quickly winning him over. Gabriel knowing in his heart that he would end up being their main caretaker, he wanted to refuse them. But between the licks, seeing how happy Simon was, and knowing the animals would be destroyed despite their heart-wrenching abandonment, he agreed to take them home.

"Do they have names?" he asked.

"The dog's name is Poohbear. The cat, that's Smokey."

Poohbear took to their two-story home immediately. Basing his decision on how affectionate Gabriel was toward him, Poohbear decided he would stay in his bedroom on the second floor. He climbed on the bed, laid at the edge, and rested his body there. Gabriel attempted to shoo him into the kitchen, but Poohbear was too excited to listen and returned minutes later.

Smokey was apprehensive. He hid under the sofa until the smell of the house felt comfortable to him. An hour later, he investigated every room and corner. Simon's room piqued his interest because he felt a peculiar aura in there. As though something other than the two masters, had been taking up the space. He decided on making the room his place of refuge.

They might be different species, but Smokey developed a set of meows Poohbear could discern. Poohbear's whines and short barks were executed at a pitch Smokey understood. They had long and loud conversations between them, followed by wild playing. Their destruction of household items and noise outraged Gabriel.

"What is wrong with you two? Why can't you two behave and stop tearing up the place? Instead of making noise, you two lazy animals need to keep the house clear of vermin and pests."

"Dad, they're playing. They're best friends," Simon said.

"Well, they need to stop making such a mess!"

Poohbear and Smokey recognized certain human words in his complaints. They agreed to have low conversations when Gabriel was in the room. Their louder talks occurred when they walked the perimeter of the home making sure nothing unwanted found their way inside. It was a routine they performed daily.

Smokey searched for vermin while Poohbear sniffed for bigger threats like would be burglars. Fortunately, in the first few years of living with the Kennedys, they never had to ward off anything more vicious than a rat.

Until the night of August 3rd 2016.

The Kennedys had gone out for the evening, leaving the pets the run of the place. Poohbear and Smokey completed their surveillance of the perimeter, entered in through the pet door and walked the lower portion of the house before retiring upstairs. Smokey went into Simon's room to his favorite spot by the window. Poohbear went into Gabriel's and curled up at the foot of the bed. Both started to nap.

Slam!

Poohbear woke first. The slam came from a door in the foyer followed by heavy footsteps in the living room. His ears perked up as he listened. Scratching resounded for several seconds then abruptly stopped. He stood, whined and looked toward the door of the bedroom. A shadow appeared. Poohbear growled.

"It's me." Smokey stepped into his line of sight.

"Did you hear that?" Poohbear said.

"I did. I got this," Smokey said.

"Sounds like something big. I'm behind you."

He followed Smokey as he slowly walked to the top of the stairs. He stuck his head through the banister columns and scanned the living room. His vision perfect in the dark. He didn't see any movement.

"I don't see—"

Smokey's ears perked as loud scratching sounds emerged from the living room. He focused on the darkness. It stopped.

"Is it a rat?" Poohbear jogged to his side and looked over Smokey's head.

"Rats don't scratch that loud. You see anything?"

Poohbear put his nose through the banister. Sniffing the air, he quickly withdrew.

"Something foul down there. Over by the big master's long bed."

"I don't smell anything." Smokey lowered his head. He focused his eyes on the dark area to the right of the sofa. The scratching resumed, and he glimpsed something move. "Hold on."

Smokey stepped away from the banister and quietly walked down the stairs. He stayed close to the wall, using the shadows as cover. When he paused halfway the scratching stopped. Smokey flexed his claws then kept moving.

Once at the bottom landing, he looked back at Poohbear who had taken position at the top step.

"Be careful, Smokey."

Smokey got low. He half-walked, half-crawled across the threshold of the living room and continued toward the sofa, growling a warning to whatever hid in the darkness.

"You're trespassing. Leave my master's house."

Smokey stopped, got into a pounce position, and waited, his tail moving from side to side like a metronome.

Poohbear licked his muzzle then began his descent. His hearing and sense of smell were heightened in the dark. He moved quickly and once at the bottom, he sensed the foul odor was coming from the foyer. He turned his attention to an open closet.

"Open door, Smokey."

"Check it out."

Poohbear approached the closet, shaking his head to clear his nostrils with fresh air before he continued his investigation. Using his snout, he pushed the door open wider and stepped inside. The smell came from a hole in the back corner large enough for him to put his head in. Caught around its edges were long strands of black hair. He slowly retreated.

"Something was in there." He headed into the living room then took position on Smokey's left. "There's a hole in the back corner." He sniffed again and barked.

"Poohbear, quiet."

"It's like garbage day on Tuesdays." Poohbear hurried over and took position on Smokey's left. His tail wagged fast as he moved back and forth nervously. He sniffed again. Barking, he stepped toward the corner of the sofa. "It's coming from right there."

"Where?"

"Heeeeere!" A raspy, demonic voice spoke from the darkness. A pale, boney hand with oily skin and sharp fingernails reached out of the dark toward the pets. The hand then bent upright and all the fingers except the pointer folded closed into the palm. A row of sharp white teeth appeared in the dark followed by a pair of red eyes above them. The creature brought the single finger to its mouth and said, "*Shhhhhhhhh!*"

II

Poohbear and Smokey stepped back quickly in unison. The creature made a gurgling sound then bolted into the adjacent dining room.

"Intruder. Intruder. Intruder," Poohbear whined.

Smokey joined Poohbear at his side. "That's not a rat."

"Smokey, back away!"

The duo scurried back to the stairs. Poohbear stepped over Smokey and used his paw to pull him close to his body to protect him. After a few seconds, Smokey let out a yowl. Poohbear answered with a bark.

"I'm okay, Poohbear." Smokey patted Poohbear's leg. "Where did it go?"

"Where the masters eat. It's in there."

Smokey stepped out from under Poohbear. "We'll have to work together on this."

"What is that thing? It feels wrong."

"Keep it together, buddy."

"I'm good." Poohbear shook his head and snapped his jaw.

"Let's go get rid of it." Smokey proceeded through the living room toward the archway leading into the dining room. "I got this side."

"Going around." Poohbear ran to the kitchen and took position at another entrance to the dining room.

Smokey spotted the creature crouched under the dining room table. He maintained his composure while silently getting close enough to pounce. He stopped when Poohbear appeared in the kitchen archway.

"I hear it. I don't see it." Poohbear looked everywhere except under the table.

Smokey turned his attention back to the creature. It had not sensed his proximity as its attention was fixed on Poohbear. It flashed its teeth as it lay flat and began to scratch the floor with its talons.

"Poohbear, look by the little master's chair," Smokey said.

Poohbear peered under the table. "Got him."

"Look out!"

The creature rushed Poohbear, pushed him back into the kitchen and tried pinning him to the floor. Poohbear growled. Barking, he fought to get back on his paws. The creature made a terrifying grumbling sound as it struggled to keep Poohbear from standing.

"Little one mine. Little one my meal. Protectors are weak and foolish," the creature said.

Smokey watched patiently as Poohbear relentlessly fought. A swipe of his paw against the creature's face caused it to let go and allowed him to slip loose from under its weight. Poohbear quickly put distance between them.

Smokey seized the moment and pounced. Landing on the creature's back, he sank his claws into its skin. The creature howled and spun in circles until Smokey was thrown off its back. He landed on all fours and slid into Poohbear.

"Get him, Poohbear!" Smokey yowled.

Poohbear barked then charged with his jaws open. The creature put its arm up to block its face and Poohbear clamped down onto it. He whipped his head causing the creature to let out an agonized wail. Poohbear used all his strength to pull and tear at its skin.

"Filthy animal! I'll eat you first!"

Smokey took to the air, this time landing on the creature's chest. He dug his claws in deep and hung on as Poohbear tore at the creature's arm. Together they forced the creature onto its back.

The creature pushed Smokey off then punched Poohbear hard in the snout. Poohbear yelped and let go. The creature stood and swiped at Smokey. The tip of its talon cut him under his chin, forcing him to back away. The creature retreated to the closet.

III

"My nose." Poohbear lowered his head as Smokey rushed to examine him. "Is it bad?"

"No worse when that prickly animal stuck you during the outdoors trip we took with the masters this summer," Smokey said.

"Did you hear what it said about the little master?"

"I heard it."

"I know what that is, Smokey. Little master said he saw something bad in his closet last week. What did he call it? You were in the hall when he told big master about it and big master said they don't exist."

Smokey scratched under his chin, nicking the cut.

"I remember. It's a monster." Smokey stared at the closet. "You said there's a hole in the closet. There might be one in little master's too." Smokey stretched. "Lets—"

The creature attacked unexpectedly. It tackled Smokey, picked him up, and threw him into the dining room. Then it turned to Poohbear and screamed.

Poohbear defiantly snarled back. He lunged at the creature to bite, but it dodged him. When it tried to back away, it slipped and fell. Poohbear attacked, locking his jaw again around its throat. The creature's skin felt soft and easy to tear.

The creature seized Poohbear around the neck and tried to pull him off, but its skin came loose in the dog's mouth. It bellowed in pain as part of its throat ripped away. Bits of flesh dropped to the floor.

But the pressure of the creature's grip grew too much to handle. Poohbear jerked away. He broke loose and landed on his back. Rolling quickly, he got to his paws and barked ferociously.

"You won't hurt little master. You won't harm our humans. I'll kill you!"

Holding its throat, the creature scrabbled to its feet and bolted for the closet. Poohbear started to go after it when Smokey ran past him.

"Get to little master's closet. I got him," Smokey yowled.

Poohbear watched as the creature disappeared into the closet with Smokey in pursuit. The cat screeched as it was tossed out into the foyer. He recovered quickly and went back inside, crawling into the narrow opening of the hole.

Within the walls of the house, Poohbear heard the creature's growls and Smokey's hisses. Poohbear followed the sounds along the stairs into the ceiling.

"The closet." Poohbear dashed up the stairs to Simon's room barking, "The closet, the closet, the closet."

Down the hall, into Simon's bedroom, he stopped in front of the closet door. He could hear the battle get closer.

"Bring it. Come on," Smokey cried.

"I'm here. Force him out," Poohbear barked.

The closet door burst open. Poohbear backed away as the creature emerged with Smokey on its face, biting and scratching. It tried to pull Smokey off, but his claws were dug in deep. The creature fell into the dresser, knocking over toys and books. It fell onto the bed, bounced and rolled over onto the floor exhausted and hurt.

Smokey let go and limped backwards. He ignored the blood that dripped from slashes to his face inflicted by the creature. He looked at Poohbear.

"Close the door."

IV

Smokey watched as Poohbear stood on his hind legs and pushed the bedroom door closed. It shut with a slam and a click. He turned and growled at the creature.

"Get up." The skin around Poohbear's teeth lifted as he snarled.

Smokey didn't wait for the creature to move. He rushed in and began slashing. The creature cried out as it swung at him. Poohbear moved in, bit its leg and dragged it to the middle of the room. Between the barks, screeching, and howls they didn't hear the Kennedys return.

"What the hell is going on in there? Poohbear! Smokey!" Gabriel called through the door.

"Daddy, they're fighting," Simon said. "Stop fightin,g guys."

Poohbear let go of the creature's leg, barking and howling as he turned and moved to the door. He jumped on his hind legs and tried to turn the knob with his mouth, but it wouldn't open. He dropped back and turned to Smokey.

"It won't open, Smokey."

Smokey ignored him as he clawed away at the creature's chest. It had lost the strength to fight back. Thousands of tiny slashes covered its face and body. Smokey didn't stop. Poohbear seized Smokey around the neck and lifted him off the creature. Smokey yowled and hissed and swipped as he was carried across the room.

When they had enough distance from the creature, Poohbear dropped Smokey on the floor and pinned him with his paw. Smokey started to calm as Poohbear lay and pulled him close like a mother cat. He began to lick Smokey's wounds.

"It's okay. We got it," Poohbear said.

The bedroom door burst open, and the lights came on. The creature faded away. Gabriel looked around the room.

"Look at this mess. What the devil were you two doing in here? I swear you leave these two alone for a couple of hours and they create havoc." Gabriel complained as he walked away. "You wanted these two, Simon, so you clean this up."

Simon entered and looked at them. He looked at the spot where the creature had been and gasped. He could see the hairs it left behind. He started to call for Gabriel but took another look at Poohbear and Smokey, who were laying in the corner. Both were battered, bruised, and exhausted.

"You stopped the monster." Simon got down on one knee and hugged them.

Poohbear happily licked him. Smokey slipped out of the embrace and approached the closet.

"What is it?" Poohbear barked.

Smokey crouched and focused on the back corner. Two red eyes appeared in the dark. Then two rows of sharp white teeth smiled, then disappeared.

"Nothing we can't handle, my friend."

Hobbs

CAT 7 PURRICANE
Kris Katzen

Times like this, Yansi didn't envy her uncle being a doctor. "Tell me," she said, when they were the only two beside her father's hospital bed. Her father had always been a big, robust man, but now all Yansi could see was someone small and frail and nearly swallowed by the medical equipment attached to him. His brother, her uncle, looked very much like her father had looked just days ago.

Monitors beeped and buzzed, and the respirator whirred. Yansi was growing to hate those sounds more and more. She looked up from where she sat holding her father's hand and locked eyes with her uncle. "Tell me," she repeated.

Her uncle's deep voice even sounded a lot like her dad's. He spoke with the same drawling cadence and melodic inflection of a natural-born singer. "He doesn't have long without the medicine. Maybe hours. At most a day or two."

Yansi nodded, silently thanking him for his honestly. She loathed platitudes and lies. The only thing she hated more at the moment was the antiseptic smell of the room and the fact that it didn't cover the smell of urine and feces in the colostomy bag. Hours, and they had a hurricane racing toward the coast.

"Don't give up. Grandma's still looking," Yansi said.

Her uncle gave a wan, mirthless grin. "I think I'm supposed to tell you that, kiddo."

At that they heard a resounding "Yes!" echo down the hall. Moments later her grandmother burst into the room, a radiant smile on her deeply-lined face. Tall and strapping like all her progeny, she effortlessly commanded any room. "I just got through to the medical center upstate. They have the vaccine, enough for all of us. They dispatched a helicopter and it'll be here in two hours."

Four hours round trip — Yansi said a silent prayer of thanks for the medical pilot, who'd be cutting it very, *very* close. "The storm is still five hours out, right?" Yansi asked. She thought it was due to hit right as the tide came in. Just perfect.

"Yes. Gives them enough of a margin to get in and out."

With the compound built high on a steep hillside, and a roof covered with equipment and instruments, the closest landing place was at the bottom of the hill a mile away. An easy ten-minute stroll.

Yansi kept glancing at her wristwatch while she sat with her father. Finally she could stand the inactivity no longer. Kissing him on the forehead, she whispered, "I'll be back, Daddy. Stay strong. You'll be fine again in no time."

Down the hall and around a bend, she stopped in her room to grab her backpack. She dumped the contents on the floor — this wasn't a rescue mission or scavenging excursion, after all, and slung it over her shoulder. This time all she needed was the medicine, and her backpack more than sufficed to hold it.

She marched through the empty gray hallways of their installation and stepped outside into the remains of what had once been a bustling port. A few skyscrapers still stood defiantly against the passage of time. From a distance, some even looked intact. The more average buildings nearby, though, the ones a mere five or ten or twenty stories, they clearly showed the damage. Few windows remained intact, portions of walls caved in. Some building leaned at precarious angles. It constantly amazed her that they hadn't yet crumbled.

Even after twenty years, the emptiness and decay — the *stillness* — still evoked the sense of absolute and total *wrongness* of the scene. Then again, what could possibly be right about the death of billions?

Thirty minutes before the 'copter was due, Yansi jogged down the hill. The road ended at what used to be a bustling shipping center. The odd crane still stood or leaned. Many of the warehouses' roofs had caved in.

Yansi stood on the two-hundred-year-old pier and looked down, way down, on the bone-dry sand of what used to be a deep-water port. Patches of dark blue-gray clouds skittered across the otherwise azure sky, their shadows racing across the ground in tandem with them. Clouds, but no sign of the helicopter bringing the desperately needed vaccines.

No rain yet, but she could smell it coming even over the smell of brine and sea salt in the air. A brisk gale tugged at her loose pants and oversized jacket and whipped her long red-black ponytail behind her. She adjusted the empty backpack straps because the wind kept blowing it sideways. Dirt and sand stung her face, and she was glad she wore her sunglasses as protection not just against the brightness, but from the particulates as well.

She couldn't tear her eyes away from the horizon. Bad enough the tide was roaring in. She could already see the mountain of water, still forty miles out, thundering in at almost forty-five miles an hour.

It would have been surging at a 'mere' twenty-five miles an hour, and she wouldn't have been able to see it so far out—if not for the hurricane bearing down on them at the same time. The black sky on the horizon defied the midday sun, the dense wall of clouds looking as solid as the water.

She sat down in the shade to wait. Hard to believe the sky was still mostly clear at the moment. But flocks of birds were flying inland, no doubt to avoid the approaching tempest. Ten minutes before the scheduled time, she got up and started pacing. Five minutes after they were due, she called back and was told to stand by, they were checking on it.

Where the hell was the medicine?

Garbage and debris blew across what had been a wide-open space where trucks and—way off to one side—trains had come and gone like ants swarming around. Now she doubted she could even find a nearby anthill—not that there were many patches of dirt among the cement. Still, back when, some city planner had planted a row of trees to divide the shipyard from the rest of the city. Some still stood in various states of tatteredness.

Where the hell was the medicine?

The helicopter should have dropped it off over ten minutes ago. Yansi needed time to get back up the hill behind her, way up the long hill, to reach their installation above high-tide level. Normally the water didn't come to within half a mile of it. For the past days they'd been moving all the most important stuff in it to the upper levels to avoid the flooding they feared was about to inundate them. Just in case.

Because the most ferocious hurricane in recorded history was blasting toward them at the same time as the highest tide of the year.

She'd already radioed back twice and each time was told to stand by. She'd give it another minute then try again. Then she was out of there, because if two-hundred-plus-mile-an-hour winds slamming her into the ruins of buildings didn't kill her, the hundred-foot-high tidal wave certainly would. She turned and looked up the hill at their shelter a mile away. Many of the buildings between her and the stone structure built into the side of the hill had begun to crumble. Half-fallen walls showed entrails of beams and girders and pipes and wires inside. What used to be a road had disintegrated into a pathway of gaping sinkholes.

Easily visible in broad daylight, the full moon peeked out from behind the hill. The moon that, as of two decades ago, appeared three times larger than it had in the past. Yansi remembered how it used to look, but barely. Back then, back before the asteroid, the moon was a beautiful, benign silver orb in the sky.

Yansi touched her earbud. "Guys, what's the scoop. I'm not seeing any helicopter incoming."

Her ear crackled a minute as the device woke the rest of the way up. Yansi recognized her mom's voice. "Yansi, you hear me?"

Her mom? Not her grandmother? Something was going on, and it had to be bad.

"I'm here, Mom. Where are they?"

"Come back now. The helicopter went down."

Yansi could hardly believe her ears. "Repeat. Did you jus— oowww!" Something bit her leg! She jumped back, away from a dark gray tabby. What the heck? But her mom was still talking in her ear even as the cat meowed imperiously at her.

"Yansi, did you hear me? The medicine isn't coming. Start back immediately."

"Roger that, Mom. I'm coming." Yansi looked at the cat, still yowling at her. "You'd better come too, you know. You can't stay here." She bent to pick up the cat, but the feline darted just out of her grasp and stopped.

Why the heck was she still there anyway? Animals had good instincts. The cat had to know the tide and the hurricane were coming in. It was a wonder the wind hadn't already blown the little feline away.

Yansi tried again to scoop her up. Again the cat evaded her, dashing just far enough away and then stopping. But the meows didn't stop. They grew more and more frantic.

"I know!" Yansi snapped, frustrated. "Come on, you little shit." No one would object to a cat in the compound. They could easily spare that much food, plus cats protected their stores from mice and rats. Very much a fan of live and let live, Yansi nevertheless realized that if rodents devoured or, worse and more likely, infected their supplies, they'd have a tough time of it.

The cat ran a few yards then waited.

Yansi's blood ran cold. Animals did have good instincts. And the cat was heading away from the hill. What if something was there Yansi couldn't see yet? They rarely had to deal with raiders or marauders thanks to the crazy tides. But that didn't mean no one was lying in wait.

But that made no sense. Yansi had been standing out in the open in broad daylight for the past twenty minutes. If someone were going to attack her, they would have. Was another quake about to hit? Wouldn't that be just perfect? On top of the hurricane and the literal tidal wave it was causing, they'd have an earthquake to contend with? Or maybe one of the buildings was about to cave in? That happened frequently enough.

"You'd better not be messing with me," Yansi growled—then followed the cat.

They started up a parallel road. *So far, so good,* Yansi thought. At least she was still going in the right direction. But then the cat went into one of the buildings.

"You little—" Yansi's anger rose.

She did not have time for this!

The last thing she wanted to do was abandon anyone to death, but if the cat refused to accept help, Yansi wasn't going to get herself killed, too. She glanced back over her shoulder. The mountain of water raced in even faster than she'd estimated before. The black strip of clouds at the horizon had tripled. The winds were increasing to gale force, howling between the buildings. It began to rain, and the fierce weather turned every drop of what would have been a light sprinkle into knife-like shards of water.

Following through the gaping hole in the wall, Yansi shifted her sunglasses to the top of her head so she could better see. Then she heard it. Even above the raging cacophony outside, she heard a chorus of high-pitched squeals.

The building had likely been a parking garage, and Yansi felt it trembling slightly under nature's onslaught. The cat stopped at the edge of a floor and started pacing back and forth, still vocalizing at full volume. Yansi went over, already knowing what she'd see. One of the beams had just fallen, crashing down thirty feet to the floor below. It had connected the floor where she stood to a ledge across the chasm, all that remained of the collapsed floor.

On the tiny ledge, Yansi could see a squirming pile of kittens. From that distance she couldn't be positive, but they looked to be under a week old, not moving far at all, which was likely the only thing that had saved them from the lethal fall.

"Are you fucking kidding me?" Yansi muttered to herself. Short of sprouting wings, what the hell was she supposed to do?

She looked desperately around but saw nothing except girders and rebar and cement and copper piping. There certainly wasn't time to call anyone for help, even if she would ask someone to risk it, which she wouldn't.

Enough of the garage remained for her to circle around, up to the level above the kittens. A ledge of floor remained there as well, along with a gaping half-moon-shaped hole in the wall that let in the pelting rain and screaming wind. She could make it, but she'd need a way down. Normally she'd have had a rope and other equipment with her, but she'd emptied her backpack to make room for the medicine. For all the good *that* had done. Then she spotted it hanging from what had once been ceiling lights.

Wiring. A bunch of copper wiring.

If there was enough of it...

She began yanking it down, exerting all the force she could. If it was going to break, she wanted it to break *now* not when she was dangling from it. She managed to liberate thirty feet of it from the ceiling. More than that refused to come loose, but that was fine. At least she did still have her knife with her. She kept that tucked in one boot no matter what.

Sharp as it was, it wasn't a wire cutter. Yansi cursed as she used precious time getting the length of wire loose. She fought the urge to sprint at top speed up the ramp and over to the other side of the chasm. The building was already falling to pieces. She didn't need to help it along.

The cat followed her but had stopped meowing. She seemed to comprehend that Yansi had understood her plea for help.

When she was directly above the kittens—she knew based on the jagged crescent-shaped hole in the wall—Yansi tugged on the pipes and beams to see where best to tie off. One section of rebar came off in her hand, nearly sending her plummeting backward.

Minor in the scheme of things, but Yansi was glad no one but the cat had heard her shriek. And she figured she could trust the cat not to tell.

More time ticked away before she finally found a reliable anchor. She secured her makeshift 'rope', lay down on her belly, and eased herself over the ledge. Climbing down was easy. She could almost have jumped the fifteen feet if not for the ledge being so small, and who knew how sturdy.

That thought made her afraid to put her weight on it. She hadn't come all this way to have her own stupidity kill the kittens.

She held tight with one hand and wrapped the wire around her waist and through her legs with the other. Somehow she managed to tie it off. All she needed was a minute or two, so she didn't care that it wasn't her best job of securing a knot. Even in the building, she could already hear that the wind outside was even louder.

She pulled her backpack around in front of her and unzipped the top of it. Six kittens, eyes not open yet. She'd been right about their age. All tabbies, but their colors ranged from darkest gray to a pale silver. With utmost care, she put all six in her backpack and zipped it shut.

Then she climbed back up, her arms burning with exertion by the time she reached the ledge. She got herself free of the wiring as fast as she could. How much time had she lost? Did she even want to know?

She been reckoning on how fast she could get back but hadn't factored in fighting the wind to do so.

"Okay," she told the mother cat, "time to go *now* and *do not* argue with me." Working fast, she tied her jacket's drawstring at her waist as tight as she could. Then she put up her hood, tied that as well, and pulled the zipper up halfway.

The cat practically jumped into her arms this time when Yansi reached for her. "Do not make me regret this," Yansi commanded, pressing the cat against her chest and then zipping her into the jacket.

Yansi made her way toward the exit carefully but as quickly as she could.

"Yansi, what's your eta?" This time her grandmother sounded over the com.

"Don't know," Yansi admitted. "Maybe twenty minutes. Maybe thirty." Now on more solid floor, she quickened her pace, still mindful of rubble, and reached up under her hood to pull her glasses down to protect her eyes.

"Yansi, repeat your eta." Her grandmother sounded incredulous.

"Twenty to thirty. Not sure I'll be able to hear you. I'll keep the line open."

Stepping out through the hole, she saw that half the sky had turned a roiling purple-black. The incoming tide was twice as close as it had been. The wind nearly lifted her off her feet, and she grabbed the wall to keep from being blown away. Taking just a few seconds, she pulled her backpack in front of her and secured it over top of her and the mommy cat. She'd be damned if she'd rescued those kittens just to have them smashed to pieces by wind or rain before they made it to safety.

Yansi braced for the pounding and left her shelter. She'd be cutting it close. She'd be cutting it *way* too close. Yansi had visions of being swept or blown away just a few yards shy of her goal.

Even uphill, she could run the distance in seven or eight minutes in normal conditions. She'd even covered the mile in six minutes once or twice. But in this weather…

She had no idea.

She supposed she should be grateful for the tailwind. She did her best to sprint, but it was difficult with the rainwater rushing down the street. On the other hand, she could feel the gale pushing her up the hill — so long as she could stay on her feet. She managed what she could generously call a stumbling jog.

She felt the mother cat pressing against her stomach, and, even with the maelstrom raging around them, she could feel the cat purring.

Nothing like a vote of confidence.

Just so long as Yansi didn't disappoint anyone, feline or those waiting for her back at the installation.

She kept one hand out in front of her to avoid toppling into anything, or to deflect any debris flying through the air. The other she kept angled in front of and above her nose and mouth to try to inhale as little water as possible. The vertical rain came from behind her, but it was coming down so hard that it poured off her.

If her backpack and jacket weren't waterproof, she feared all the cats would already have drowned.

They still might, herself included, if she didn't get it in gear and reach her destination. Despite her gut screaming at her to go faster! faster! faster! Yansi forced herself to slow down just a little so as not to fall.

It was all she could do to stay on her feet. If she lost her balance in the raging flood, even though it wasn't yet deep, she'd be swept back to the bottom of the hill and maybe even off the pier.

One stumble and they were all dead.

Good incentive to tell her gut to shut up and listen to her head so they didn't get killed.

Then again…

Gallows humor made her laugh. When she got back inside, her family would likely kill her anyway for doing something so foolish and scaring them so badly. A risk she'd have to take, she told herself. She refused to do it for them.

Of course she might not have to. Without the medicine, they might all die. She'd have to find out about that once she was back if they could send another helicopter after the hurricane passed. She hoped the pilot who'd gone down had survived.

She cursed the weather over and over.

They still desperately needed the medicine.

Her father had gotten sick two days after getting back from his trip to bring back some much-needed equipment. Two days of exposing all the rest of them to the virulent, deadly flu before he knew he had it. Normally, staffing the science station on the coast kept them all safe. They hardly got any visitors. There were far easier places to attack for food or other necessities. There was nothing to see but reminders of the catastrophe that had ravaged the whole world. The tides made the location an inaccessible island for half of every day.

But as far as monitoring seismology and meteorology went, they had a prime location. So her grandparents ran the place. A number of other family members had followed them into the sciences and also leant their expertise. At last count one hundred thirteen of them lived there: both sets of her grandparents, twenty of her parents' generation, and the rest grandkids and great-grandkids.

They had plenty of room since it had originally been designed for five hundred personnel. Now their skeleton crew did its best to collect as much data as possible and disseminate it to the rest of the world.

"If you can hear me," Yansi said, even though she highly doubted they could, "I'm halfway up the hill." The higher she got, the more the flooding decreased. I'll be coming in the south gate. Repeat, coming in the south gate."

The wider other street led directly to the east gate.

Knowing her grandmother, though, she'd have people watching for her and manning all three gates.

So strange that the sky directly overhead was still blue. All the rain came from the storm front behind her, yet the overhead had not yet clouded over. Sun glare made it hard to see. Yansi laughed at the preposterousness of it, then regretted it because of swallowing so much rain. Just two blocks ahead, or what used to be blocks when the buildings had still stood, she'd get to the crossroad that ran in front of their compound.

Her legs burned and her whole body hurt from exertion.

From the outside, their compound looked very much like an old warehouse.

Inside, however, it overflowed with state-of-the-art equipment, updated from what had survived two decades ago.

Glass shattered nearby, and Yansi wondered if any windows were still intact. Bigger and bigger objects flew through the air: pieces of trees, pieces of cars, pieces of buildings, pieces of who knew what. She finally forsook keeping water out of her face by grabbing up the metal lid of an old trash can and holding it behind her. Thus far she hadn't been pummeled by anything big enough to knock her down. She didn't trust her luck to hold, however, as she saw more and more stuff sailing by. She felt more than heard some heavy objects hitting her makeshift shield. And she felt the ground beginning to tremble beneath her feet.

Yansi almost missed the other cat clinging piteously to the rubble rushing past. She gave herself a mental slap. Not that she'd had any time to search—if she'd even known where to begin—but of course mommy cat hadn't made those kittens alone. Not slowing, she grabbed him just in time.

In those few minutes, the maelstrom of black clouds filled the sky overhead. Finally reaching the cross street, she only had to traverse the length of a football field to get to safety. She risked a look over her shoulder.

Her heart nearly exploded in her chest, and she wished she hadn't looked.

Even through the driving rain, almost black as the clouds directly above, she could see the entire ocean rushing toward shore.

Yansi suddenly feared they'd all be washed away. She turned, dropped her makeshift shield, and sprinted like she never had before, finally able to run with the ruins now partially blocking most of the wind.

As she got close, the heavy metal door opened, and her uncle waved her inside. As if she needed more encouragement.

He heaved the door closed behind her, the sudden lack of noise from the rain and wind nearly deafened her with its silence. Giving him the side-eye, he took the half-drowned cat from her.

"The surge," Yansi gasped, doubled over with hands on her knees, "The surge! How big is the surge?"

"Approximately a hundred feet," her uncle said, putting a steadying arm around her shoulders.

"A hundred feet?" Yansi tried to do the math, but the image of the water kept intruding.

She stood and pushed back her hood, noticing that a lake of her own making surrounded her. Her mind raced as she stepped out of the puddle and clutched her uncle's arm with one hand as she yanked off her boots with the other.

The pier itself was fifty feet. Their compound was half a mile further inland and the elevation another five hundred feet. She nearly fell over with relief. "Ok, so we should be good. What happened to the helicopter? Did the pilot make it?"

"The helicopter cr—what the hell is that?" her uncle exclaimed, voice rising and eyes going wide with shock.

Mommy cat appeared, pushing her head up to see out from the jacket. She popped up from inside her makeshift taxi compartment and peered at her new surroundings.

"Another cat," Yansi said with mock asperity, willfully misunderstanding. "What happened to the helicopter? Grandma said it crashed."

Yansi stifled the urge to shake the answer out of him. It looked like her uncle had to concentrate hard to focus his attention on the question. "Yes, it went down—got caught in a crosswind. The only good thing is, the pilots are fine, and they saved the medicine too. As soon as this storm breaks, they'll get it to us."

As soon as the storm breaks. Yansi understood what her uncle left unsaid. If the storm didn't break soon enough, they'd lose her father.

She could hear the storm through the thick cement walls, but only if she listened for it. It didn't compare to what she'd experienced outside.

Yansi would happily have ridden out the storm without any anxiety if not for her dad's deteriorating condition. With their own generator chugging away as reliably as ever, there was no risk of losing power. Water wasn't an issue either, even when storms weren't dumping foot upon foot of rain. And they always had supplies enough to last them at least a year.

The only thing they lacked was the medicine.

They needed it as fast as possible because as hale and hearty as they were, when any of her grandparents started showing symptoms, they wouldn't last nearly as long as her father. The smallest children were also at far greater risk than a healthy adult. Although none of the children were permitted in the hospital area at the moment, chances were quarantine was already useless. Symptom-free when he'd returned, her father had had plenty of contact with everyone.

Rapidly recovering from the shock, her uncle now regarded her with a raised eyebrow. "You know we're going to kill you, right? You saved two cats? What the hell, did you chase them a mile in the opposite direction or what?"

In answer, she opened the top of the backpack so he could see inside.

He looked at her, at the kittens, back at her, back at the kittens, handed her back the cat, and rolled his eyes then walked away.

"You are so dead," she heard him toss back over one shoulder. But she also heard his voice shaking with laughter.

She took solace—and diversion—in setting mommy cat and the six babies up with their own corner of her room. Daddy had his own space in her bathroom since the kittens were still so tiny. Just to be safe, she kept the door locked to keep out the smallest children since they didn't yet understand how delicate the tiny kittens were.

The tempest raged on all night and all the next day and night, the only respite the hour when the eye passed directly overhead.

Close to sunrise, Yansi was sitting with her father when the radio went off. "Can you hear us? Repeat, can you hear us, WS13?"

"This is WS13," Yansi replied. "Go ahead."

"Apologies," the low raspy feminine voice, said. "Our radio went out and we just got it back. We got your medicine and we're on the ground."

She barely dared to believe what she was hearing. "Please repeat. Confirm your location!"

The woman rattled off the correct coordinates then added, "We're at the docks, just waiting for you."

Yansi let out a "whoop!" and jumped to her feet. "Do not move, I'll be right there." Then she leaned close and kissed her dad's forehead.

She didn't know how he was still alive, but he was fighting every inch of the way. "You hear that?" she said. "The medicine is here. I'll be right back with it. Do not go away. Do you hear me, Daddy? Do not go away."

She ran full tilt out of the room and down the hallway, making everyone scatter to get out of her path. She shouted a few times that the vaccine had arrived, took the stairs one landing at a time, and shot out of the building as if out of a canon.

"You brought back how many cats?" her dad fixed her with a stern look across the dinner table. He still looked too pale, and Yansi saw the occasional tremor, but he was well on the way to a full recovery. With the vaccine administered, no one else showed any of the symptoms.

At the moment the only ones eating besides her and her parents were two younger cousins. They started giggling, not fooled any more than Yansi was.

"Eight. We now have mommy, daddy and six kittens."

Her father's fierce façade crumbled into laughter. "You are a crazy woman," he said. "We really should kill you, you know, for a stunt like that." A serious glint came into his eyes beneath the humor. "Do not do that again."

"I won't if you won't," she told him.

Rigel and Kris

SUCH INDOMINABLE SPIRIT
Danielle Ackley-McPhail

THERE IS A HARSH TRUTH ABOUT LIVING ON THE STREETS. BE IT CAT, DOG, or human. It comes with scars. Sometimes they are physical, sometimes they are reactive. And yet even with the hardship faced, there is a will to survive.

A while back a cat friend began to frequent our yard. A big buff boy who sadly appeared blind. He would come and go, sunning himself, at ease, until we ventured near. We never could get close without him panicking away. We assumed that his blindness came from battle scars, an unfortunate but common occurrence in the wild as strays protect their territory. He had adapted well to being blind and got around with no problem. Otherwise, our friend—whom I dubbed Samson—seemed in good health and clearly was being fed.

He came and went and apparently felt safe enough to chill on our patio furniture from time to time, even relaxing enough not to completely run away if we came out for some reason. We were always careful not to move too fast, always greeting him with low, soothing tones when we knew he was near. It was clear he came to recognize our voices, but was too skittish to let us get close.

We kept a watchful eye out, and were concerned about Samson's health when we noticed some kind of seeping left behind on the cushions. Since we had been unsuccessful getting close to him, we reached out to animal control, having learned our local shelter is a no-kill shelter.

They caught him fairly quick and we found out two things, our neighbor down the street had been feeding him (and was very distressed when animal control came out to take him away) and we later learned he'd lost his eyes due to ear infections so bad he'd inadvertently scratched out his own eyes.

The community rallied around Sampson, with the shelter receiving donations specifically for his care. His damaged eyes were removed, his infections treated, and ultimately, my neighbor not only adopted him, but kept his name!

I am able to visit from time to time. He still recognizes my voice and even comes close enough for me to touch.

Samson living his best life, safe inside and going where he pleases.

HIDE AND GO SQUEEK
Eric Hardenbrook

"Hey, mister, why are you out here?" The young man strolled up to the ramshackle table set up beside the door.

"Yeah," added the girl walking with him. "Why aren't you in there, where the rest of the books are?"

The man shifted and his folding, portable chair squealed in protest. "I am out here because I get to see all the customers before they even get inside. How much better can you get?"

"Sure, I guess. But it's hot out here in this weather, or humid. I forget," the girl squinted and looked up.

"Yeah, and it looks like it might rain," added the boy.

"Well, I have my portable shelter with me as well," the man gestured up. His shelter looked vaguely like four umbrellas that had been poorly stitched together.

"I guess," the boy didn't sound convinced.

"Well, I'm not here to talk about the weather or shelter arrangements, I'm here to sell my newest book!" the man waved his arm in grandiose fashion across the stack of slender volumes arranged in front of him. "I'm the author of these fine…"

Just as he was about to launch into his sales pitch the door swung open between him and his potential customers stopping his conversation.

Jay, the other author present for the signing event was holding the handle of the door while chatting with a couple just leaving. "Thanks so much for dropping by folks. Thanks again, I'm sure you'll enjoy all three of my new books. Be sure to stop back and tell Michelle what you think of them." Then he turned and went back into the store pulling the door closed behind him.

"Hey, mister, who was that?" the girl asked.

"That was Mr. Smith. He is the other author here for the signing today. Now as I was saying…"

"Yeah, but he's inside," the boy followed on the girl's thoughts.

"Yes. Yes, he is. So is that stupid cat."

"OH! We love the cats!" the girl gushed. She missed the attitude that radiated from the man sitting there.

"Yeah, totally. They're so cool that they climb and get to go wherever they want," the boy looked envious.

"What particular cat do you mean?" The girl asked.

"Squeekie, of course," the author continued. "It's the only one that's always here! But I don't want to talk about that, I want you to see the book…" and the door opened again to stop the conversation. Smith shaking hands and waving folks off with another copy of his book.

"Squeekie is our favorite!" The boy started again as soon as the door closed.

"Yeah, he's so cute I just want to hug him," the girl hugged herself and twisted back and forth for emphasis.

"He is not cute. He's constantly trying to climb all over me. It doesn't matter when I come in or where I try to set up." The author slumped back into his portable chair. "The very first time I came in for a signing he clawed a hole in my pant leg trying to get in my lap."

"Well, just pick him up. Duh." The boy seemed less than impressed with a single hole in a pair of pants.

"I will not. I don't like cats."

"How do you write books if you don't like cats?" The girl raised a single eyebrow in question. "I thought that was like a requirement or something."

"NO, it most certainly is not." The author leaned forward warming to this new subject. "Cats and all other manner of pets are a nuisance. They distract from the actual writing."

"No they don't. Ms. Michelle has a whole book of stories about her cat." The boy waved at the poster on the door. "And she keeps a bunch of other ones until they find their forever homes."

"Yes, that's all well and good for her, but I don't like them. I didn't much like the hole in my pants, but I could let that go. The second time I came in I set up in front of the door where Mr. Smith is now. No sooner was the table level than the cat's up there getting in the way and knocking over my soda."

"Oh, you know he didn't mean that, he probably just wanted to help." The girl glanced wistfully at the door. "I really like playing with the cats when I'm here. Sometimes I don't even look at the books," the girl looked ashamed, as if that were some kind of crime.

"That's my point…" and the door swung open between them again. A group of three older children walked out holding copies of Smith's latest book.

"Look, will you two please move a little closer to me over here?"

"Sure, but you wouldn't have this problem if you were inside." The boy didn't seem to notice the glare that comment earned him from the author.

"I was inside for that signing. I couldn't keep anything standing upright on the table. That cat kept knocking everything over. IF he wasn't knocking things over he was yowling and laying down on top of everything."

"Cats don't yowl; they meow." The girl smiled while she closed her eyes doing her best impression of gloating when one knows the answer and others don't.

"That one yowls. So I moved my table for the next signing. I went to the table back by the bathroom. That wasn't any better — the cat was back there constantly." The author's consternation at reliving the whole scenario was beginning to turn into a sour mood.

"Well, couldn't somebody pick the cat up for you?" They both seemed to think that was an excellent solution.

"Yes, we tried that. The next time I was in I called ahead. I asked them to give me a spot near the shelves holding the staff picks. I thought that would be a much better solution. As it turned out the cat simply leapt down from one of those boards that run all over the place and tried to land on the diagonal shelf. That didn't work entirely as the cat planned so he caromed off that and onto me again."

Both the boy and the girl giggled. "I bet that was funny," the girl added.

The author crossed his arms. "Hardly."

"Well, that still doesn't explain why you're out here," the boy said.

"I tried a table by the door. I tried a table in the back. I tried a table by the shelves up front. No place I went seemed to work." The author leaned forward and put an arm on either side of the table. "So the next time I came into the store I sent a text ahead again. I asked Michelle to let me use a spot in the expansion area toward the back of the store. She was happy to oblige, but no sooner did I set up my little corner back there than that darn cat poked its head out of the shelf right next to me and tried to climb onto my shoulder! I even brought my own daughter to the store so she could occupy the cat. Squeekie wanted nothing to do with her—wouldn't go near her."

"Wow, he really likes you." the girl sounded so in awe the author couldn't shout his reply at her.

"Yes, but as I stated before I don't like him."

"You should, it would be easier." The boy seemed determined.

"It would not. In fact I took part in another signing day when the tables were all downstairs in the basement and within five minutes that cat had tracked me down there and was knocking things off my table!" The author was red faced and sweating. The humid weather was starting to get to him.

"Oh, we don't like the basement it's super creepy," the girl shuddered.

"I like it even if you don't," the boy puffed his chest out. "I went down there during one event, and they turned the lights out on us for a whole five minutes," he went on proudly.

"Yes, it's a wonderful and creepy space but still plagued by cats. Now, however, I have won our little game of hide and seek. I am here and he can't get out to torment me. Listen, I'd like to tell you about the books I've got here…" and once again just as the author attempted to describe his work the door swung open.

"There you two are. Would you please come inside?" A kind-looking lady waved her arm at the children, "Come on! We don't have a ton of time today, and besides, it's starting to rain. Let's go!" She smiled and both of the children turned and trotted into the store.

"Good luck, mister," the girl waved and pulled her arm back in just as the door swung shut.

The author blew out the breath he hadn't realized he'd been holding. *How could one miserable cat be such a ridiculous bother?* He glanced up as the patter of raindrops began on his shelter. He heaved another deep breath and shifted his table a little deeper beneath cover.

Just as he thought he might be safe and the rain a passing shower a stiff breeze swept across the parking lot and the downpour began in earnest. He glanced up at his shelter while he warily slid some plastic over the top of his books. So long as the wind didn't get out of control he'd be just fine.

As soon as the thought crossed his mind the door swung open and the mother of the two children he'd been chatting with came back out. Her back was to him as she leaned against the door handle and pushed her umbrella out and open. "Come on you two, I told you we didn't have much time," she was waving the two children back out to the parking lot. The boy dodged out to the leading edge of the umbrella immediately sticking one hand out into the rain. The girl was close behind and turned her head to look back into the store. That's when the author saw the cat. It was Squeekie and he was making a dash to escape. The author stood reaching out a hand toward the door.

Just like a movie, the actions of everyone slowed down in the author's mind. The little girl turned and bent to stop the cat from getting out. Her mother spun awkwardly in an attempt to both keep her son reasonably dry and out of the rain while reaching back for her daughter. She backed up a half-step, pushing the door past normal extension. The door knocked into the front leg of the makeshift shelter.

Just as the author shifted and looked up to judge the possible damage the sagging patch in the center of his little roof gave way and dumped the puddle of rainwater directly onto his head. The chilly water made him roar in frustration. He slapped his hands down on the plastic covering his books to save them and turned his now-dripping head back toward the door.

In the moment he glanced back he saw the cat stop. Just stop and sit down on the floor. The family bustled out to their car completely oblivious to the author's plight. The author sighed and ran his hands back over the top of his head to push some of the water off of his face. At that moment the cat stood up, turned, and walked away from the door as if to say, "my work here is done."

"Fine," the author grumbled as he stuffed books back into boxes. "You win today, cat, but I'll be back and next time I'll figure out a place to sign where you won't be able to get at me."

GETTING TOO FAMILIAR
Charles Barouch

THE CAT WAS A FEW WEEKS OLD WHEN I FOUND HER. BEDRAGGLED AND abandoned in the alley behind my apartment building. My building as in I rented there, I owned close to nothing.

I worked two jobs. Barely had enough to feed myself. Still, I didn't hesitate. I took the tiny kitten in and made her part of my life. She paid me back in cuddles and scratches. Plenty of both.

In the odd hours when I wasn't sleeping or working, I wrote. At first it was just the occasional short poem any time inspiration struck. Since little Spatter had joined my household, I found myself attempting longer pieces.

She'd crawl across my desk, upsetting my papers and pens. It should have upset me, the breaks in my concentration that she caused, but it never did. I started thinking of her as my writing familiar, doing for my fiction what a wizard's familiar did for their mystical arts.

One morning, after I lost the catering job, my side hustle, and money was especially tight, I woke to find that I'd no memory of getting into bed. The lack of food and the abundance of worry had put me in that sorry state. Something had to change. Sooner the better.

I looked at the pages I'd written the night before. There were more than I recalled. Many more. It was an entire play, three acts, narration, stage direction, all of it.

Spatter jumped onto my chair and nuzzled my leg. I dropped the papers when she spoke.

"Good, isn't it?"

"I'm hallucinating."

"Not a surprise," she said. "You've been eating so little. I feel bad for you."

"Cats don't talk."

"But we do eat. And you've been feeding me even when you go hungry. I wanted to pay you back."

I gave up on fighting the lunacy of the situation. Rolling with it, I committed to the conversation.

"You wrote this?" I asked Spatter.

"Good, isn't it?"

"But I wrote this. I recall dreaming up Melody's character. And Frank's."

"You wrote Audrey from across the hall into it and called her Melody. And Frank is exactly you. Well, you as you see yourself."

"So you admit I wrote this."

"No, I admit you wrote part of a draft of one scene. I rewrote that and then, I guess I got carried away. Did the whole thing in one night."

"And you think scraping my play for yours is paying me back?"

"Literally. The Little Playhouse will give you a hundred dollars for that minimum. So, paying you back, literally."

"You put my name on it, Spatter."

"Yeah, speaking of names, can you stop calling me that?"

"Your fur pattern looks like you're a white cat that someone spattered with black ink."

"So I should call you weird beard? Since we're naming each other by fur patterns and all."

I scooted the cat off the chair and sat with my head in my hands. I needed to eat. That would help me clear my mind. Help me stop imagining conversations like this. How wrecked was I that I was debating the origin of a play with my cat?

"Not going to ask?" she said. "Not going to ask my preferred name?"

"Your name is whatever I chose to make it."

"A name is just the noise you make to get someone's attention, *Greg*. If I don't answer to it, how is it really my name?"

"Then your name is psss, psss, psss. You come when I make that sound, Spatter."

The cat put her head in the air as if to say she was disgusted with me. She walked away into the kitchen. I went through the pages of the play. It wasn't bad. And, I had to admit, it wasn't mine. I'm not this good. Not yet, at least.

"Hey, Spatter," I called out.

She didn't come.

"Psss, psss, psss," I tried.

No dice.

"What's your name?"

"Ahpuch," she said as she trotted back into the room.

"Look, ahpush…"

"Ah-putch," she corrected me. "Like putch with a barely voiced 't' in it."

"Great. Ahpuch it is. Pleased to meet you," I said. "I have a question. What makes you think the Little Playhouse will buy it?"

"They have an open-market call for plays," Ahpuch said.

"And you know this because?"

"Hang on, Bobby. You can buy into my using the computer to type of a play and print it out but the idea that I can google has you disbelieving?"

"Fair point. So, you're a cat. And a playwright. And a computer wizard."

"Not a wizard," Ahpuch said. "That's not my role. Not ever."

"Apparently, I've offended you…"

"*Again*. You've offended me again, *Bobbby*."

"Right. Double apologies. Triple if you need'm. Look, I'm too wrecked to argue. I'll just call the Little Playhouse."

"Call? They put an ad online, I bookmarked it. Just go to the ad and respond like a person from this century."

"Etiquette lessons from a cat. Great."

The computer was already on. I opened the browser and found the bookmark. The site loaded to reveal an ad for Little Playhouse. So, either this was all part of the same dream, or the cat was telling the truth. That might have been the weirdest thought I've ever had, awake or asleep.

I uploaded the document and filled out the details on the form. For better or worse, I just sent my cat's play out with my name on it. Okay, that was an even weirder thought. Great. Wonderful.

I stumbled into the kitchen and opened up a can of food for Ahpuch. Then I checked the fridge. I still had two cups worth of iced coffee in a pitcher. I poured some and sipped it slowly while I tried to decide between the two-day-old salad and the three-day-old half sandwich. I settled for both cups of iced coffee and no food. I'd need what's in there to get through tomorrow.

I still had my main gig, driving for a car service. Can't do that if I'm not safe to drive. And that's where my life was now. Eating was a reward for going to work. It's not something I could afford to do on days off.

If the play got bought, I could to treat myself to pizza on a Tuesday. I don't work Tuesdays. One sale, assuming I even got that one sale, wouldn't really change anything.

"I'll split the can with you," Ahpuch offered.

"I'm not quite up to eating cat food, but thanks."

"Your loss. This is quite tasty."

"Hey, can I ask you something, cat? Why don't you ever finish all the food. Why do you always leave some?"

"Because I can."

I took a nap despite having just gotten up. It's easier to not eat if you're sleeping. The caffeine from the coffee didn't interfere. The roiling of the coffee in my otherwise empty belly did. I couldn't get my eyes to stay closed. I sat in my chair and petted Ahpuch until she started biting.

"Why do you do that?"

"I bite you, but you'll still pet me the next time, won't you?"

"Yeah."

"That's why. Here's what you don't seem to get, Bobby. When doing the thing you feel like doing has no negative consequence, there's no reason to not do it. I leave food, you still feed me. I bite; you still pet me. I cough up all over your rug, and you forgive me. So, why shouldn't I?"

"That's borderline evil, cat. We should be kind for the sake of being kind. You're saying that as long as you suffer no bad effect, it doesn't matter if others suffer for you actions."

"Correct. Now, how about you let me get back on the computer. I feel a short story coming to me. And that magazine you used to get, Fantastic Digest, has a contest."

"How do you know about the magazine? I haven't bought one in years. You haven't been with me that long."

"You have some in the back of your closet. You shouldn't go look; I pooped on them last week."

"Because you can?"

"You got it, Twinkles. See, I'm calling you by something that's not your name. How do you like it?"

"Just fine, Spatter."

"I told you not to call me that."

"Why not, cat? I doesn't do me any harm."

"You know what, Twinkles? I'll give you that one. Pretty sharp."

I watched the cat hop up on my desk and start typing. She had her claws out. Only way for her to hit only one key at a time. I sat for a bit and tried to close my eyes. It didn't work any better than lying down did. Curiosity took me over to my desk to see how the story was going.

I had to admit, the cat had a certain style. She wrote like I did, only a little bit better. Her dialog was tighter. There's a better economy of words. Not terse, not sucked dry of adjectives, just... I don't know, better. The cat probably would know the right way to say it.

"Don't read over my shoulder. This is only a first draft, Twinkles."

"Where else should I be, Spatter? There's the empty kitchen, the empty bed, and the empty chair."

"Take a walk. Take two. Just leave me to get it all down. You can see it once I've done an editing pass."

I got dressed and went to the library. That was my life today, chased out of my apartment by my own cat. Six days a week of driving and I got to spend my Tuesday off loitering at the library.

Not that I dislike the library. It's just that I spent the rest of the week being told where to go and when. Tuesdays should be different. Right?

When they closed the doors, I checked out the book on Mayan pottery I'd been reading. Not my favorite topic or anything like that. The little I'd read over the cat's shoulder included a mention of Mayan artifacts. Seems like Ahpuch was even choosing my reading materials.

When I got home, there was pile of papers on my desk. The cat had even placed my blue pencil on top of the stack.

"Have a go at it, Twinkles. It needs some more edits but I'm tired. Not good for a cat to be awake more than four hours a day. I'm not a kitten anymore."

"You pretty much are, Spatter."

I started reading. It was trash. I mean, the words were arranged into sentences, and everything seemed to be spelled correctly but it was a wandering mess.

I abandon the printed pages and got on my computer. I made a copy of the story and started editing that. Rewriting, if I'm being honest. Trimming out whole sections. Moving things between chapters. I didn't like a lot of Ahpuch's choices. The main character was what I call plot-stupid. If she were smarter, the story would work differently. I start wising her up.

When I was done, the general idea remained, but barely anything of the cat's draft did.

"Hey, Spatter!"

The cat walked in, clearly drowsy. I must have wakened her. A small, crazy part of my brain wondered if she was using up all the sleep and that's why I was awake. And yes, I get that I'm considering that crazy while fully accepting the notion of a cat who talks, writes, and edits.

"Woke me up. Better be good, Twinkles."

"How did you write such a good play and follow it up with such a crappy story?"

"Where'd you learn those manners?" she asked me. "If I wrote a good story, you wouldn't have had anything much to do, right? You don't expect me to do absolutely everything for you, do you?"

"You wrote a mess, so I'd fix it?"

"Writing's a muscle, Bobby. I left you with some exercise."

I couldn't argue with that. I headed to bed. This time I did get some sleep.

The next morning I picked up my neighbor's car. I leased it from him so I could keep my job. The car I used to use, my car, has been in the shop for a month. It took only two days to fix the quarter panel, but he wouldn't return it until I finished paying off the work.

That's the fun thing about being poor. You end up owing everybody something. It's almost like life is set up to keep you on your heels.

When I got home, Ahpuch looked annoyed. Like seriously pissed. I thought back. *Did I scoop the poop before I left? Yes. Did I feed her? Of course. And yes, there was water out. What did I do wrong?*

"Out of printer paper and ink," she said.

"I made thirty in tips. Should have been four times that, even with what the company takes."

"Your company steals from your tips?"

"People tip on the app. Credit cards incur processing fees. And I get taxed on all of it because it's not in cash."

"Your life sucks, Twinkles. Anyway, I left you another crappy short story and I pooped in your sock drawer. Have a good night. I'm going to get some sleep."

I headed for the computer. Damned if I was going straight for the sock drawer. Day's been shitty enough. And yes, I'll own that pun. Word play? Whatever it was, I said it.

The story was a train wreck of a tale about a wrecked train. I dove in. Working on it helped me forget that I'd already eaten my only meal of the day.

When I took a break, I realized I'd been at it for hours. I didn't take time to change out of my work clothes. I didn't refresh the cat's food or water. Good thing she was sleeping.

I went to the bathroom, got comfortable, and did my chores, before remembering that the half sandwich wouldn't last another day. So I had a second meal, as it turns out.

Checking my e-mail, I saw I had a 'we've received your play' message from Little Playhouse. Form letter, nothing to get excited about. I sent off the story from yesterday. I hoped Fantastic Digest would like it.

That left me wondering where I should submit the new one. I noticed there were two new bookmarks. It seemed the cat had been looking up markets.

The alien abduction at the core of the story I just rewrote made it perfect for one of the sites she'd marked off. I considered the other. Maybe I could wing it and try to make a story for them without Ahpuch having to start me off. What the hell, why not.

The reason why not was that I ended up pulling an all-nighter. I didn't have that sort of stamina when I was well fed. Not with six to eight hours of driving ahead of me. Good thing it was my short day. If this were a weekend, I might be doing twelve hours behind the wheel.

I did my — cat and non-cat — chores before I left. When I got back, the cat looked happy. Other than illustrations for Alice in Wonderland, this could be the first time I'd ever seen a cat grin.

"Little Playhouse said you made it to the second round of consideration, Twinkles."

"How would you know… Spatter, have you been reading my email?"

"Dummy, I curl up in your dirty clothing pile. It's pretty clear I have no consideration for any of your boundaries."

"This has been going on too long to be a delusion, cat. I think I have to admit that you really talk."

"And inspire your writing, and claw up your best shirt…"

"You ruined my…"

"Yes, the cowboy shirt. Honestly, I did you a favor. That thing was hideous."

"Since you've been in my email…"

"I'm not your secretary, Twinkles. Read it all yourself."

I refilled Ahpuch's bowls and cleaned up a little before I settled in at the computer. I found the email the cat had mentioned. Round two, not a yes, but not a no. I didn't have anything back from the magazine, but I'd only sent that off yesterday. It was surprising that Little Playhouse had turned things around so quickly. I couldn't expect anyone else to be that overly prompt.

There was an email from Max. I hadn't heard from him in over a year. We'd lived together for about four months and then we had that fight. He thought I was flirting with Lindy, the waitress I used to work with in catering. I wasn't. Well, not seriously.

The weird thing was, it didn't read like the start of a new conversation. It seemed like he was responding. I scrolled down until I saw that he was doing exactly that. My busy-body little kitty had sent him a message from my address.

I would have been livid if it weren't for the fact that Max seemed interested in getting back together. That bought Ahpuch a lot of forgiveness. Still, it felt like a cheat. I didn't want to build a second chance on dishonesty.

But, what was I going to do? Email him saying that my cat wrote the message? That wouldn't scare him off, right? Telling him my talking cat liked to impersonate me online? Sigh. Double sigh.

I found the cat asleep on my bed. I considered waking her but didn't. Nothing I was going to say was that urgent. It was probably better if I thought it all through before having that conversation. And yes, that's where my life was… rehearsing what I might say to my cat.

It dawned on me that I'd written an entire short story in one sitting. That'd I'd done an extensive rewrite on another the day before. I was pretty sure that most professional authors did four thousand words or less in an average day. This pace was unsustainable. Despite that, once I was done with my email, I started to write.

The cat had bookmarked those two sites. One would get last night's story. I started working up something for the other one. It was a weird science fiction sort of online magazine. I had no idea how you made money doing those, but they claimed to be paying SFWA-level rates. I started with the idea of having someone with synesthesia — a condition which create sensory confusion — who used that as an asset in communicating with a plant from outer space.

All the poetry and short stories I'd done were deathly serious, brooding stuff. This one was fun, silly, fluffy. It might have been the first time writing didn't feel like work. I dug in. My exhaustion fell away. And that was a bad thing.

It became a second all-nighter. Two in a row on too little food. I did two hours of work and then called out sick. My boss was royally ticked. The line they throw you when you start is that you are your own boss, that you work as much or as little as you want. And maybe that's true in other cities or other shifts, but not with my boss. I took off anyway.

I'd already had an accident in my car. I wasn't going to drive exhausted in my neighbor's. That wasn't just consideration for him, mind you. If I wrecked his, no one would lend me another. I'd be out of a job, and I was already down to just one of those when I really needed two.

I came home to find Ahpuch's puke in three different rooms. I didn't have it in me to be upset. I cleaned it up even though all I wanted to do was sleep. When I was done, I looked around for the little furball. There was no sign.

I needed to collapse. Instead, I filled her bowls and ate the wilted salad. My fridge was officially empty of solid food. There was a half-bottle of cranberry apple something, two pickle jars that only had brine left in them, and that was it. The freezer held a significant buildup of ice and an exploded can of soda.

Having ditched work today — mostly ditched work — I wouldn't be filling the fridge anytime soon. I sat down and wrote for six hours. It was becoming an obsession.

I heard a knock at the door just before dawn. It least I thought I did. I was exhausted and the sound was pretty faint. When I pulled the door open, Ahpuch waddled in with an envelope in her mouth. She dropped it at my feet like it was a prize catch she was showing off to me.

"How'd you get out?" I asked her.

"Ask a better question."

"What's in the envelope?"

"Six thousand dollars, Twinkles."

"How?"

"I wrote a ransom note. They are the best word-rate payout of any writing."

"You what?"

"It's a joke, Twinkles. I picked the lock on the mailbox and got this out of it."

"Who's mailbox?"

"Yours, idiot. Keep up."

I picked up the envelope. It felt thin. I looked at the return address. I knew the name. It was an up-and-coming studio. They started out making web shorts two years ago and they'd graduated to making… I want to say nature documentaries.

I opened it and saw a check. I blinked, hard, and looked at the check again. Six thousand dollars. I'd wonder how the cat knew the exact amount but having six thousand dollars was weirder to me that having a talking cat who could guestimate dollar amounts.

There was a letter inside. I read it. Then I read it again.

"Ahpuch, why is Natty Filmworks paying me an option fee?"

"Oh, I sold them the rights for your first novel. Well, just the rights for the first year. If they don't make a movie by then, it all reverts. And, technically, you own the copyright either way, so… it's like that."

"I haven't written a novel."

"Technically, no. I wrote it. If it helps, I did base the main character on that grim-dark poem you wrote the night you took me home."

"Okay. Okay. Okay. Let's say for a moment that you wrote an entire novel. And edited it. And, all the other stuff one does. Wouldn't it have to be published to be optioned? Published, reviewed, sold… sold a lot of copies. Don't those things usually happen first?"

"Yeah, well the thing of it is, Twinkles, I wrote it two years ago."

"You aren't two years old, Ahpach. And you can stop calling me Twinkles. I'm using your real name."

"I forget how linear humans are. I read your poem two years ago. That's my timeline. You wrote it less than two years ago. That's your timeline."

"So you've been writing under my name for how long?"

"First one published six, no… seven years ago. Didn't sell well but it established your name. That's why Little Playhouse responded so quickly. You're a good get. A name that might sell some extra tickets."

"How do I not know that I'm a multi-published author?"

"When was the last time you bought a book? Other than my chasing you to the library, when was the last time you were there?"

"Fair enough. But if I've been — you've been — publishing for six years…"

"Seven, Twinkles. Seven years. If you're asking about the royalties, why would they go to you? I did the work, right? It's nice of me to drop the six k in your lap. I don't owe you any of it."

"You have a point. Not my work. Just my name."

"Let me lay it all out for you, Twinkles. You've had a rough go of it. Consider me karma, trying to balance your account a little bit."

"So there's what? An army of karmic cats out there righting the wrongs of the universe?"

"No, just me. But I'm polyphasic and out of sync with the general passage of time, so I have a lot of opportunity."

"So you're here fixing things up for me and also in a dozen other homes at the same time?"

"Pretty much. I'm glad you read science fiction. This is so much harder to explain to the non-fiction crowd."

"Great. Can I ask why I was chosen?"

"You rescued me, remember? It all starts with kindness to someone who you think can't help you back. You fed me when you were hungry. That means something."

"But there are other kind people."

"I'm not omnipotent. I can only help where I happen to be. I'm polyphasic but not omniphasic. I can't be everywhere. And, to be honest, none of this is on me to fix. You didn't save every cat, you saved me. That's how it works. We help where we can and hope the little things we do somehow make the big picture things work."

"Wow. That's a lot to take in. So, this money, I get to keep it? Is that how this works?"

"Twinkles, you do, but there's one more thing I haven't explained."

"What's that?"

"Cats can't write fiction."

"But you…"

"Stole these stories from the future you."

"How does that even work?"

"Look, it's been great, Twinkles, but I can't stay and explain. You're on your path. I'm off to help others. Just do me a favor? Anything you write in the next three years, just put it under that floorboard and forget it. It's all already been published, and the payments will start coming in. Don't screw yourself up by trying to sell it as new work. It'll be new to you but reprints to everyone else."

"You're leaving?"

"See, that's your good heart, Twinkles. I'm talking about your future, and you're still focused on me. I'll miss you. I'll look in on you. But right now, I have to go."

"Where?"

"A guy named Gary Gygax is about to double down on his commitment to be an insurance salesman. I have to steal his future game designs and get him started on his new path. If I don't, he'll spend his whole life thinking AD&D only stands for accidental death and dismemberment."

Patches

NEXT-LEVEL CAT RESCUE

As we've already mentioned, cat rescue can be a difficult, often thankless job, but have we also mentioned how heartbreaking it can be? This isn't just about getting cats off the street, or fixing them before letting them loose again. Oh no… there are so many other worst-case scenarios.

Life and death situations—sometimes for both the rescue and the rescuer.

We won't go into too much detail because you aren't here for a degree in cat rescue, but we wanted to touch on some of those situations that most people don't know are a harsh reality of cat rescue life.

Bottle Babies

There are times when rescue involves kittens too young to be away from their mother. Either the mother has been found dead, is too ill to care for them, or for some reason has rejected her kittens. If a surrogate cat mom is not available the kittens must be placed with an experienced fosterer knowledgeable in bottle raising kittens.

Not only will they require feeding every two to six hours, depending on their age, but they are very delicate and helpless when young. They cannot regulate their own temperature, they cannot poop or pee on their own, and they must be fed kitten milk replacement formula. Other types of milk can cause serious health issues.

It is touch-and-go when trying to bottle raise kittens, but sometimes there is no alternative.

Special Needs Rescues

It is not uncommon to find ill, injured, or special-needs cats in the wild. Sometimes this results from lack of proper care, sometimes from abuse or accident, or are conditions the cat is born with, though these rarely survive long in the wild.

Such conditions can be expensive for a rescue or shelter and may ultimately result in the animal being put down. Some rescuers will only resort to such steps when there is no hope of returning the animal to a decent quality of life where it can either be returned to the wild if feral, or adopted if that is not an option. Unfortunately, special needs cats are difficult to adopt out.

Hoarders

Cat rescues will often be called in by the county to collect animals from a hoarder house. Generally in such situations the animals are not receiving proper feeding or medical care, the living environment is unclean and or unsafe, and the animals have not been neutered. As the section title implies, there are an unreasonable number of cats — and often other types of animals — being kept under less than ideal, health-threatening circumstances. This can pose a danger to the animals and the rescuers.

Big-Cat Rescue

Yes... you read that right. Whether being held as pets under less than ideal conditions, used in illegal animal fighting, escaped from zoos, or found injured in the wild, there are big cats out there requiring rescue/capture. Say a prayer for those rescuers out there who specialize in big cats. Believe it or not, other than the need for tranquilizers and special equipment, this isn't much different than domestic cat rescue, just on a larger scale... and with an increased risk factor.

If they are wild animals that have been injured they receive medical care and are tagged and released. If this is not an option, or their injuries are such that they cannot be reintroduced into the wild, there are zoos or wildlife refuges where they can live out their lives safe and happy and cared for.

DEGLOVED
Brad Jurn

COLD AND HUNGRY, THE LITTLE BLACK-AND-WHITE KITTEN CREPT OUT OF
the field and toward the farm below. He smelled so many scents that
made his belly rumple and clench that he ignored the musky odor he
knew meant danger. Crouching at the edge of the grass, he spied two
large dogs. One paced the yard sniffing the ground and the air. The
other sat on the porch, ears pointed and swiveling, tongue lolling
between sharp white teeth.

Neither noticed him.

His belly to the ground, the tuxedo kitten crept forward toward the
barn where he smelled the sweet aroma of milk and mice. Another
rumble. His belly, or the dogs? He stilled and his head whipped around.
The dog on the porch scramble to his feet, the other dog gave a low
woof.

Too hungry to retreat now, the cat scurried for the barn, the dogs at
his heels, barking. His heart pounded as he scrabbled up the ladder to
the loft, their teeth snapping at his paws. For a while they paced below,
their muzzles pointed toward his hiding spot, huffing low growls. He
sat huddled among the hay just beyond the edge of the loft, too afraid
to even look for mice.

He half-dozed, his eye drifting shut, but his ears perked to catch
any sound of threat. Eventually he heard the *tip-tap* sound of the dogs'
claws fade away as they left the barn. Crawling back to the edge of the
loft, he peered down. They were gone.

The ground. It was so far. But his belly screamed louder. Gathering
himself, he leapt down, but in his haste to follow the scent of food
he caught his paw in a crack in the worn concrete. He cried out. He
couldn't help it. The hard surface pinched his foot and held it tight,
no matter how he tugged. He cried more, frantically tugging even

harder as he heard the scrabble of the dogs' claws and their renewed barking.

The cat panicked and threw all of his weight in the opposite direct, trying to pull himself away with his other three paws. As the dogs neared and the saliva flew from their teeth with each bark, the cat flung himself back even harder, ripping himself free leaving a trail of blood behind him as he dove into a nearby ditch and hid in a plastic underground culvert. The tube was too narrow for the dogs to enter, but their barks echoed after the cat as he hobbling out the other end of the pipe.

Climbing out of the culvert beside a dirt road, the injured cat limped along the shoulder, meowing frantically. A cloud of dust arose in the distance, as a car slowly approached. Tommy tried to run down the side of the road but could only hobble, his little heart pounding once more as he cried. The car, however, came to stop beside. A young woman quickly climbed out and slowly approached him with her arms outstretched. He hissed and spat, swatting at her with a leg missing its paw. She cooed and murmured nonsense at him while a man exited the car with a blanket in hand. The cat tried to dodge away, but the people gently scooped him up. They wrapped him in the blanket and brought him back to the car, though he continued to hiss and growl.

They Googled for the nearest animal hospital. The closest available was the Chicago Drive Veterinary clinic only five miles away. The husband called ahead to inform the clinic that they were bringing in a wounded kitten with a missing leg. The clinic staff told him they'd be ready, and to try and stop any bleeding. The couple sped down the road making yet another dust cloud, in the hope of saving the wounded kitten before it was too late. The kitten offered little resistance as the newly wed Cara Tomlison wrapped its wounded leg in the handkerchief she had her hair up in. She looked to her new husband, Dave, and said in a trembled voice, "I hope she doesn't bleed to death!"

Dave looked to his wife, then to the kitten. "Just wrap it tight, and he should be fine. They'll stabilize him when we get there."

"It's just a clinic. Will they be equipped to handle this?"

"Yeah, I think so. It said emergency services available."

Upon arriving at the clinic the Tomlisons were met in the parking lot by an Asian woman wearing scrubs. She was holding a blanket in one arm and a cat carrier in the other. Cara quickly exited the vehicle and handed the now frantically meowing cat to the veterinary technician. The Tomlisons followed the woman inside.

The wounded cat was quickly rushed back to surgery and the Tomlisons were greeted by a receptionist. "Are you the gentleman I spoke to on the phone?"

Dave nodded. "Yes."

She looked to each of them. "Is this your cat?"

"No," Cara responded. "We were driving to our new home and we just happened to see him limping down the road. He's probably a stray."

The receptionist nodded. "I'm sure Dr. Coll will check to see if he's chipped after surgery. It's not uncommon for strays to wander in the country. He may have also live on a nearby farm, probably attacked by another animal. This kind of thing happens a lot in rural areas."

Cara looked to her husband and then back to the woman. "Do you think you'll be able to save him?"

"I think you got him here in time. I'm sure they're stabilizing him right now. Once he's stabilized, Dr. Coll will make the decision whether to amputate the leg or not."

The Tomlisons looked to one another, then back to the receptionist. Cara asked, "We've been thinking about adopting a kitten, actually. If she…"

"*He…*" Her husband cut in. "I saw it's a he."

Cara looked back to the tech with a smile. "Okay, if *he* makes it through this, what are the chances he'll make a full recovery?"

The receptionist smiled back. "Lots of animals who are degloved…" At their puzzled looks she clarified, "lose forelimbs make full recovery. Most are unburdened at all by a missing leg or foot. It just takes some rehabilitation and time."

The Tomlisons looked at each other with a smile. "May we wait here until the surgery's done?" Cara asked.

"Sure. It may be some time though before we have any information. But you're welcome to wait in here in the lobby."

"Good," Cara said. "Thank you! We're *just* getting back from our honeymoon, and we're beat."

The receptionist's face beamed. "Oh, wow! Congratulations!"

"Thanks," the Tomlisons replied. "We haven't even made it home yet to unpack."

"Well I think it's really nice that you two came to this little guy's rescue. He would have probably died if you hadn't found him. Please have a seat on the couch and I'll let you know his status as soon as I hear anything."

The Tomlisons seated themselves on the comfortable leather couch and doodled on their phones for a while. It wasn't long before they fell fast asleep.

"Excuse me." A warm voice awoke the Tomlisons. "I'm sorry to wake you. But we're done with surgery." They looked up to see a middle-aged woman with sandy brown hair wearing scrubs looking down at them. "We were able to stabilize your stray."

Cara rubbed her face sleepy face. "Stray?"

"We scanned for a chip and didn't find anything. My guess is he's a stray, or perhaps a feral, who's been separated from its mother." The doctor reached out to shake the Tomlisons' hands. "I'm Dr. Coll."

The newlyweds sat up straight and shook her hand. Dave asked, "Will he make a full recovery?"

Dr. Coll nodded. "I believe so. I decided it was best to amputate the entire leg. What was left might have been more of a burden."

"A burden?" Cara asked.

"Yes. More often than not, cats in this situation will try and use what's left of the leg, which results in more injuries, sores, and infections."

Dave straightened on the couch. "Is he in any pain?"

Dr. Coll smiled. "Not at all. He's under sedation, and we've stabilized his vitals. He'll be on painkillers and monitored throughout his recovery, but I believe he'll make a full recovery."

Cara scrunched her face. "Even with a missing leg?"

Dr. Coll smiled. "Yes, even with a missing leg. He may be a bit wobbly at first, but after some physical therapy to prevent further injury and to help him regain his balance, he should get around just fine."

Dave looked to his wife, then, back to the doctor. "What if we wanted to adopt him once he recovered? If he's a stray would we have dibs?"

"Well, once he's..."

"*Tommy...*" Cara cut in. She looked at her husband, then back up to the doctor with a smile. "While he was in surgery we couldn't help giving him a name."

"Great!" Dr. Coll replied, with a warm smile. "But as I was saying, once we're through rehabilitating him here, he'll be transferred to Michele's Rescue to start the adoption process. There'll be a stray hold period of about three to five days to make sure no one's looking for Tommy. Our chip scan was negative, so you may be in luck." Rather than continue standing over the couple, Dr. Coll sat next to Cara on the couch and continued. "Next, they'll give Tommy all the necessary vaccinations and monitor his wound. Once he's deemed fully recovered he'll become eligible for adoption. You'll probably be interviewed by an adoption counselor to make sure you're a good fit for Tommy and his handicap." A smile spread across her face. "Something tells me that won't be an issue."

The Tomlisons smiled back. Cara reached out and gave the doctor's hand a squeeze. "Thank you for saving him. We weren't sure if he was going to make it."

Dr. Coll put her hand atop Cara's. "Sweetie, it was you and your husband who saved him. You should both be proud. Now why don't you leave Tommy to us so you two can go home? I hear you have a honeymoon to unpack from!"

The Tomlisons looked at each other and smiled with tired eyes.

During the weeks of Tommy's recovery Cara called the clinic periodically to check on his progress. In the third week the Tomlisons were finally contacted and told they could come in for a visit. The receptionist, Kristie, met them in the front lobby with a hopeful smile, leading them to a room reserved for appointments and cat playtimes. Kristie left the Tomlisons alone momentarily to retrieve Tommy. They held hands as they waited, and took in the small room. Cat toys covered the floor, and a scratching post sat in the corner.

Kristie returned with the young tuxedo cat cradled in her arms. His wide eyes looked at the Tomlisons with curiosity. Kristie gently lowered the kitten to the floor, and he awkwardly leaned forward due to his missing appendage. as she watched Tommy slowly bring himself upright with the support of his front leg. Cara covered her mouth and gasped when Tommy started to make his way to them, only to stumbled forward and hit his chin on the floor. She quickly rose from her chair to assist the struggling kitten, but Kristie held up a reassuring hand. "He'll be alright. He's still learning how to adjust his weight and balance with the missing limb."

Tommy straightened once again and hobbled toward the Tomlinsons, who were now both sitting cross-legged on the floor. The young couple smiled as the young feline limped closer to them, letting out little mewls. He went directly to Cara, who gently lifted him and gave him a loving cradle. "Poor little guy," she said, as they sat there petting him. Tommy's eyes narrowed and he let out a low purr he soaked up the love of his rescuers.

Cara teared up as she smiled at her husband. "Dave, we're bringing him home, I don't care what it takes."

"I'm sure the clinic will put in a good word for us with the rescue. Besides, if anyone deserves first dibs on Tommy, it's *us*. We rescued him."

They continued to pet the purring kitten, who was now almost asleep. After a few minutes Kristie returned. She smiled as she entered the room and saw the Tomlinsons sitting on the floor. Cara cradled Tommy, who was now fast asleep, and Dave held his wife.

"How was your playtime?" Kristie asked.

Cara looked up. "I honestly think he just wanted to be held."

Kristie sat in the chair against the wall. "Yeah, we had him out already this morning with the other kittens. He kept up with them pretty good, but he's still learning how to balance with limited mobility. Before long he'll learn how to fully function without the front leg."

Dave looked up at Kristie. "Do you think he'll *fully* recover and walk normal?"

"Oh, sure!" Kristie answered. "Tripod animals can sometimes be even faster than four-legged cats because of their cantered gait. That means they can build speed faster because they have one less limb to slow them down." The Tomlisons looked at each other surprised. Kristie continued. "Once he's fully adapted to three legs he'll be just as resilient and quick as a four-legged cat. If you're planning on adopting, you might want to make sure your home is equipped for a tripod pet."

"Equipped?" Mike asked.

"Yeah, you'll want to have as many rugs and carpeted surfaces as possible for less slips and falls. The more traction the better. I would also recommend getting low-sided litter boxes for easy access; same goes for bedding. I wouldn't recommend having him as an outdoor cat either. Tripods are much more vulnerable than animals will all four legs, as they can't climb or protect themselves very well."

"Thanks," Dave responded. "We're already planning on making the house as safe as possible for Tommy. The stairs are already carpeted, and we'll make sure he has easy access to food and water. I was also going to build some 'cat stairs' at the end of our bed in case he wants to sleep with us at night."

Kristie smiled. "You'll want to mention that to Michele's Rescue when you go through the interview process for adoption."

"About that," Cara inquired. "Is the adoption process any different for an animal that's been degloved as opposed to a four-legged one?"

Kristie shook her head. "Not at all. They'll just want to make sure Tommy's going into a safe and suitable home, which you're obviously going to provide." She reached over and patted Tommy's head, and he gave a slumbering meow. "They may want to do a home visit, but it sounds like you'll be more than prepared." She looked to the young couple with a reassuring gaze. "And Doctor Coll and I are planning on giving you a two a really good reference when he's transferred to the rescue. He'll even be neutered and immunized before we release him. So all you two need to do is let Tommy here continue his recovery, and we'll let you know when he's ready for adoption. After that you'll fill out an application and set up an interview."

"Wow!" Mike exclaimed. "You make it sound like a done deal."

Kristie smiled. "In *this* case, I think it's safe to say it is."

Elsa Mari Cunningham the Third

FLUF

F.R. Michaels

"Good evening, Miss Barrow," said a voice from out of the darkness.

Amy Barrow shrieked and jumped, her keys and groceries tumbling to the floor. She whirled and spotted the silhouette of a man sitting in her club chair in the dark. Amy darted for the bed across the studio apartment and groped underneath, but found nothing.

The intruder snapped the light on. Amy turned. The man matched his voice perfectly: tall, elegantly dressed in a cloak and sharply-creased suit, with bushy black brows and a salt-and-pepper goatee. He was bald but for a fringe of graying hair that draped past his shoulders, and his eyes were glittering points. In one hand, he held a gleaming black walking stick with a faceted quartz orb at its head that sparkled and shone distractingly. In the other, he held Amy's Louisville Slugger with his thumb and forefinger, as if he found holding the bat distasteful.

"Looking for this?" the cultured baritone called out.

"Get out of here right now!" Amy shouted, pointing to the door. "Get out of my apartment or I'll call the police!"

The intruder bobbed an eyebrow. "No need for that, Miss Barrow. You and I merely have some business to attend."

"I'm calling the cops."

Amy yanked out her phone and thumbed the screen.

"That is not going to work," the man said. There was a sonorous tone to his voice that burrowed through Amy's ears and into her brain.

Amy pressed 9-1-1 but the phone would not connect. No bars, no WiFi; the phone merely displayed a swirling wait animation. Amy went cold. A strange man had invaded her apartment, whom she'd walked right past in the dark, and she found herself without weapon or means to call for help. Yet he sat there in her chair, regarding her calmly, not making any move toward her.

"How did you get in here?" she asked, trying to keep her voice from shaking.

"The door was open, so I let myself in."

"The door was locked and bolted. The door is always locked and bolted." *Even now,* Amy thought ruefully.

The man shrugged. "There are doors, and there are *doors.*"

"I'll scream," Amy threatened.

"No, you won't," he said with a little shake of his head.

Amy filled her lungs and… nothing. It was as if she'd forgotten how to do it. She expelled the air but no sound would come out.

The man said, "You may speak, if you use your 'inside' voice."

A little hiccup escaped Amy's throat, and she could talk again.

"How… how did you do that?"

"Magic," he replied, with a negligent wave of his hand.

"Look, just take whatever you want and go."

The man made a quick scan of the room. "There is naught here worth taking, honestly, except one very specific thing. And if I could have simply taken it I'd have done so before you had returned."

"What? What thing?"

The man pointed with a pursed-lipped glance and his black walking stick.

Sitting disinterestedly on one end of the sofa was a runt Persian cat with a lazy left eyelid, resembling not so much a cat as some amorphous clump of black fur that had accumulated over time through some unfathomable process. Amy, inspired, had christened him Fluf.

"The *cat?*" she asked incredulously. "He's just a stray I took in a few weeks ago. Is this about the ad I put online? Is this *your* cat?"

"No," he stated flatly. "I do not own a cat. Nor am I ever *online.*"

"Then what?"

"My familiar. And I've come to get him back."

Amy stared, speechless. The intruder stood.

"I'm afraid I've been very rude," he continued, sauntering toward her. "I've not introduced myself. My name is Anton Krull. I am a warlock."

Amy suddenly felt cold. *This guy is a nutcase.* "A wh-what?"

"A warlock. A male witch."

"No, I know what it means. Don't... don't come any closer."

The intruder laid the baseball bat against the wall behind him and did a slow circuit of the room, inspecting the titles on her bookshelves and occasionally picking up a photo or figurine then replacing it with a dismissive grunt or *pff!* Of disapproval. All the while he spoke in his sonorous voice.

"I am actually trying to help you, Miss Barrow. You have no idea what danger you are in."

Amy swallowed, sweat breaking out on her body. "I have sort of an idea," she murmured, more to herself than him.

She matched his movements around the room, keeping the maximum distance between them in the cramped apartment. If she could circle back to where he'd left the Louisville Slugger, she could end this home invasion in her favor.

Anton tried an easy smile that landed between somewhere between harmless and crazy. "You won't need your club, my dear. I intend you no harm. The threat was here already. What you have unwittingly let into your home is no cat."

"No?" Amy peeled her eyes away briefly to glance at Fluf, who fastidiously licked his crotch with a little pink tongue.

"No. That is the earthly manifestation of a creature of the Nether Planes, which was bound to me by the covenants that link a warlock and his familiar." He pointed with his stick again, careful not to touch. "This is the demon Sholoth-Uul."

"Sholoth-Uul" paused from his crotch-licking to swat at his own tail.

The intruder continued. "I see you do not believe me. No matter. You may hear the truth from his own lips." To the cat, he commanded, "Speak, demon. Show this unbeliever your true self."

The cat blinked once, but, of course, said nothing.

The warlock blew an impatient breath from his nostrils. "Do not play games with me, demon. Speak, Sholoth-Uul! I command you to speak!"

The cat looked from him to Amy, then back. "Mrrrowrrr...?"

"Um, excuse me, Mr. Krull," Barrow quavered quietly, trying to sound reasonable, "but you must have made some mistake. That's Fluf. He's a *cat*."

Anton appeared about to say something, then scowled. "'*Fluf*?'"

"Yes. Fluf."

Anton shook his head and came to her laptop and printer. His attention caught, he picked up a sheaf of papers from the printer, his eyes scanning.

"'The Witch's Revenge'?" he read aloud. "Are you a writer, Miss Barrow?"

"Um, yes. Well, trying. It's my first novel, supernatural romance."

Anton said nothing, scanning pages, reading. Vanity overcoming fear, Amy Barrow sought his face for a reaction.

"What, um, what do you think?"

He dropped the papers, rubbing his fingers as if he'd just held something distasteful. "Vapid."

Amy Barrow felt as if he'd struck her. "'*Vapid*'?"

"Yes, vapid. Dull, flavorless..."

"I *know* what it means! How is a story of witches and black magic and supernatural revenge *vapid*?"

"What would *you* know about witches and black magic? You've had a demon under your own roof for weeks, now, and you're feeding it cream, rubbing its ears, and calling it 'Fuzz'."

"'Fluf.'"

"Whatever. And I have made no mistake! I've gone through a lot of trouble to track down this treacherous hell spawn, after we'd been, mm, *separated*."

"Separated?"

"I died," he admitted with a grin.

"Um, looks like you got better," Amy said cautiously.

"Previous incarnation," he explained with a wave of his hand. "Burnt at the stake for practicing sorcery back in the year of your Lord 1690-something. To this day I cannot abide the smell of barbecued meat. While I was gone, Sholoth-Uul took the opportunity to desert me." He chuckled. "I'm afraid I am a rather harsh taskmaster, and given to fits of unreasonable temper, but he and I have been together through countless incarnations, over centuries. Whatever his grievances, they do not release him from his obligation to me."

A kernel of resolution formed in Amy Barrow. For her own safety's sake, she'd play this weirdo's game, but there was no way she was going to hand little Fluf over to this admittedly abusive psychotic.

"If you *are* this powerful warlock," she said, "and Fluf *is* your familiar, then explain again why you didn't just take him and leave before I came home."

"For the same reason I don't simply kill you now and take him," he replied amiably. "Really, Miss Barrow, for a woman with ambitions to write about black magic, you know frightfully little of the Dark Covenants. Defection among familiars is rare, but not unknown. Sholoth-Uul came here, to you, during that time in which he was free of my will."

Amy screwed up her face, trying to follow. "Like, imprinting?"

"Something like that. Only your command can release him to his rightful master."

"You."

"Me."

Barrow shored up her courage. "So you need my willful co-operation?"

"Sadly, I do."

"If I refuse?"

He smiled. The sight of it froze her like a frigid wind. "I will be forced to, ah, convince you."

"I see. So what happens after I've commanded the demon-cat to return to you? When you have no more need for me, who's seen your face and knows your name, and could identify you to the authorities?" She forced the next question out. "What happens to me then?"

The irritating superior smirk that Anton wore fell off his face, leaving something cold and empty its place. The mask only slipped for a second, but Amy felt the danger. She sensed that to Anton Krull she did not even register as a person, only an obstacle to what he wanted, and that scared her more than anything.

"I, ah, if I have my familiar back, I would have no need to hurt you. I would consider giving you a reward for your, ah, help."

Liar, liar, cloak and pants on fire, Amy thought.

While he'd toured the room she'd orbited carefully in the opposite direction. The Louisville Slugger was propped against a wall just few steps away. Amy memorized its position with her peripheral vision, keeping her eyes locked on the intruder.

Anton frowned thoughtfully and turned away. "I had hoped to conclude this amicably, Miss Barrow."

"Yeah, me too," Amy said.

She took a quick jump back. Grabbing the baseball bat, she lunged for the intruder. Her foot came down on an aerosol can from her spilled groceries. The can rolled under her foot, her leg shot out at an awkward angle, and she fell heavily against the hardwood floor. Her knee twisted painfully and she lay there, groaning.

"Careful, don't slip," Anton said as he turned around.

He bent over and picked up the can.

"Kills ants, roaches, and other insect vermin on contact," he read, tossing it aside. "Useful."

He crouched down to look Amy in the eye.

"No more foolishness. If my intent were to hurt you I've had plenty of opportunity. Give me what's mine, and I will be out of your mousy brown hair."

Amy hissed with pain. Anton offered her a hand up, but she batted it away. He stood and watched her gain her feet with effort. She pulled up the baseball bat and, with a furious growl, cocked it back to swing.

"That bat's too heavy for you," Anton said in his sonorous voice.

The weight of the bat suddenly became more than Amy could lift. Its sudden mass pulled her arms down the floor and nearly took her with it. When she bent and tried to retrieve it, it wouldn't move; it was as if it were cemented in place.

Anton watched her with a hint of a gloating smile on his lips. "To be honest, the whole 'primitive with a club' aesthetic didn't suit you, Miss Barrow, being a literate woman and all. Maybe try your phone again?"

Anton snapped his fingers. She pulled the phone from her pocket and saw she had full bars and WiFi. She pressed 9-1-1 and put the phone to her ear, watching the intruder the whole time. The phone purred on the other end and picked up.

She said in a rush, "Hello, my name is Amy Barrow and I need the police there's an intruder in my apartment and…"

No sounds came from the other end: no greeting, no operator.

"H-hello?"

Inhuman screams blared from the phone into her ear. Amy pulled the device away from her and stared at the screen. Baleful demonic eyes stared back. As she recoiled in horror a small skeletal hand reached out from the screen and slashed at her face. Amy yelped in terror and dropped the phone.

"Wrong number, I suppose," Anton quipped.

"Wh-what is happening? Is this a dream?" Amy slapped her own face, trying to wake herself.

Anton chuckled. "No dream. Now kick that phone device away from you."

Amy hesitated. Suddenly the screams were right behind her, all around her, and she could feel the ghostly skeletal hands clawing at her clothes and flesh. She shrieked and kicked the phone away. Her injured leg gave and she collapsed to her knees. Her heart pounded in her chest and her pulsing blood roared in her ears. She felt cold all over, fear locking into her veins like an encroaching frost.

Anton crouched down again.

"Do you believe I'm a warlock now?" he asked her. "I have powers, Miss Barrow, real powers, not just these little parlor tricks you've seen so far. You do not want to displease me any more than you already have." His eyes stabbed into hers like knife points. "Give. Me. Back. My. Demon."

Amy glanced at Fluf. The little cat looked her in her eyes and gave her a slow blink.

"No," Amy said.

Anton let out a gust of breath.

"Very well," he said. "I'm afraid it's time for the convincing part."

He reached out and pulled Amy up roughly by the hair. She yelped and clutched his wrists to get him to let go, but Anton's grip was iron. She fought desperately, and they slammed into her desk, upending it, spilling the laptop and papers to the floor, along with the fluttering pages of her novel. He wrenched her into a choke-hold. Pulling her to the kitchen area, he dumped her roughly into a chair. All her adrenaline and panicked thrashing were no match for his size and physical strength. He grabbed both her wrists in one powerful hand, and with the other he yanked the electrical cord from the coffee maker. Amy struggled and cried out, but to no effect. In seconds he had tied her wrists behind her back and to the spokes of the chair back. Amy squirmed and pulled against the restraint, but that only made the electric cord cut into her wrists.

"Stop this," she said, sobbing. "You're sick, you need help. Let me go! There's jewelry in the dresser, just take it and leave!"

"I didn't come here for charm bracelets," Anton said, breathing heavily from his recent exertion. "I came for one thing, and I am not leaving without it. Command Sholoth-Uul to return to me."

"You're wrong," she said. "There's no demon, Fluf's just a cat. He does cat things. Why do you even need a familiar, anyway? What do they even do?"

Anton leaned back and raised an eyebrow. "Do? Why, they assist the witch or warlock with their spells and incantations. They can shape-shift, locate objects, retrieve information. Most importantly, they protect their masters from threats of both the nether planes and the mundane one." He shook his head. "Don't you know this? I thought you were writing a witch story?"

He turned to the stove and lit the front burner. Blue flames popped and danced into the air. Anton went to the knife block and selected a heavy chef's knife. Amy watched, terrified, as he laid the blade over the flame.

"It is not too late to stop this, you know," Anton said as he watched the blade heat up. "Just one single command. Tell the demon to return to me."

"I'll scream," Amy threatened. "Your magic won't stop me this time. I'll find a way, I mean it. I'll scream."

Anton grabbed a dish towel and carefully lifted the knife from the burner. The blade glowed red.

"Yes, Miss Barrow," he said. "I'm afraid this time you will."

He approached Amy, his face as resolute and pitiless as a stone gargoyle. Anton paused in mid-step. Fluf had wobbled over, and with an awkward jump had landed on Amy's lap. He turned and looked up at Anton.

"Mrowwrr?"

Anton froze, the heat of the knife smoldering the edge of the dish-towel.

"What is this?" he murmured.

A flash of insight flitted through Amy's brain. "Do you think the, um, demon will let you hurt me? Oh, yes, I know he's really a demon. He, um, he speaks to me. At night. Fluf, I mean, Sholoth-Uul is my familiar now. I'm his rightful master. He won't let you harm me."

She expected Anton to scoff, but the man hesitated. It looked as if some sort of understanding passed between the man and the runt cat, one that left Anton uncertain. He broke the gaze and looked back at Amy.

"Do – do you have any idea what you're talking about?"

"Yes. Maybe. Do you really want to risk it?"

Anton shifted his gaze to the cat again, and took an uneasy step back.

Amy sensed a ray of hope in this dark night's tunnel. "Mr. Krull, what if we struck a bargain?"

The question took the warlock aback. "What do you mean?"

"You want your familiar back. What if we do a deal? You give me something in return, and I'll command, um, Sholoth-Uul to return to you."

"What kind of deal?"

"You're a warlock, right? There are covenants and contracts that you can't break, right? Something like that?"

"There are."

Amy spoke with increasing confidence, sensing her words were reaching him: "Let's you and me enter into a contract. I will return your familiar to you in exchange for a service you will provide to me, plus the assurance that you will do me no harm, physical or magical, ever again."

Anton stood there, thinking, then turned and placed the hot knife in the sink. He leaned against the counter top. "What service would you ask of me? Riches? Love? Power?" He snorted. "Beauty?"

"Rude." Amy shook her head. "None of those."

"Then what?"

"Teach me."

Anton blinked. "What?"

"Teach me. Teach me some magic. A spell, an incantation, something so I know all this is real. Something simple, something I can use. Something I can put in my novel."

"You're serious," Anton marveled.

"I've never been more serious about anything in my life."

"And you'll return Sholoth-Uul to me?"

"Scout's honor," Amy said. "For real, I was in the Girl Scouts."

"I am not surprised," Anton quipped. "Very well. A bargain it is. We'll need a clear space, as well as candles and some salt."

Fluf meowed his agreement.

Anton untied Amy. She rubbed the welts in her wrists ruefully, and stood on shaking legs.

The made a space in the main room, Amy pushing the baseball bad and aerosol can to one side. She found some candles in a junk drawer from the last blackout, and pulled a bottle of whiskey from under the sink.

"Oh, we don't need that," Anton said.

"You don't," Amy replied shakily. "I do."

"It would best if you keep a clear head," Anton said, watching her pour a triple shot of the hard amber liquid into a tumbler.

They set up a magic circle in salt on the floor, three candles burning around the edges, Anton sitting in the "north seat" as he called it and Amy sitting opposite him in the "south seat" with her glass of whiskey. The lights were out and they sat illuminated by the dancing candle flames. Fluf, or Sholoth-Uul, watched the activity with interest at what Amy figured would be the "south-west-cat-seat." He had to be restrained twice from batting over the candles.

"This is kind of exciting," Amy said.

"Calm your mind," Anton intoned somberly. "Invoking the spirits isn't some parlor game, it requires the clearest thought and focused intent."

"So what do we do first?"

"Since you are a neophyte at this, you must empty your mind. Lose all you think you know, forget your sense of self, open your thoughts to the vastness of the spiritual realms."

"Okay."

"Now, to make sure you hold to our bargain, we will do the contract first. You have the square of paper from the printer I asked for? With the exact words, written in black ink?"

"Uh, yeah, right here. 'I, the undersigned, will adhere to the letter of this contract, yadda-yadda-yadda, I will return the demon Sholoth-Uul to the command of the warlock known to me as Anton Krull, upon completion and proof of successful magical procedure taught to me, Amy Barrow, dated and signed.'"

"Do you have the pin?"

"Yeah, I dipped it in the whiskey."

"Thumbprint in blood at the bottom."

Amy jabbed her thumb with the pin. "Ow. Okay, here you go."

"I will do the same, right there. Now, we burn the paper and the words and submit them to the spiritual ether."

He touched the paper to the candle and held it carefully as it burned.

"I think I'd like to summon an elemental spirit," Amy said, watching the paper burn. "Those are a thing, right?"

"Yes, elemental spirits are a 'thing.' That's a little advanced for your first time, though. What type of elemental did you have in mind?"

Amy reached behind her while Anton Krull observed the burning paper.

"How about *fire?*"

Amy whipped the aerosol can from behind her back and sprayed a heavy mist of pest-killer through the burning paper onto the warlock. The stream erupted in a gout of flame that enveloped the intruder, setting his clothes and beard on fire.

Anton Krull screamed in shock and terror, flames catching on his clothes and hair. He dropped the paper and swatted at the fire desperately. Amy dropped the aerosol and dashed her glass of whiskey on the burning man. A second gout of flame roared up the front of Anton's thrashing body. He rolled and shrieked as Amy stood and picked up her Louisville Slugger. She lifted it in her hands as if it were as light as a magic wand.

"Here's some magic for you, you bastard."

Amy slammed the end of the bat like a bayonet into his midsection, knocking the wind from the smoldering warlock. The second blow came down across the back of his head. Anton Krull grunted once and lay still.

Amy threw her duvet over him to smother the remaining flames, just as her smoke alarm went off.

It took the police eight minutes to get to Amy's studio walkdown, where they found Anton Krull awake but dazed, bound, and gagged. She'd opened all the windows to let the smoke out. The burlier officer looked at the warlock's face.

"Oh, we know this guy," he said. "Anthony Corelli, also known as Anton Krull. Used to do a Vegas hypnotism act. Claims he has real magic powers."

"Magic powers and two outstanding warrants," the other officer, a policewoman, said.

"Looks like you got him in custody without our help," the first officer said.

The two officers pulled Anton to his feet. He responded angrily, but no one could understand him around the ball-gag. Pink frilly handcuffs bound his wrists.

"Um, yeah, I'm going to need those back," Amy said.

The policewoman shrugged and shook her head. "We don't judge."

When the ball-gag was pulled from his mouth, Anton turned to the cat, who regarded him coolly from beside Amy's feet.

"This is your doing, you treacherous hellspawn!" he growled. "You know I cannot conjure with my hands bound!"

"Hey, hey, hey, pipe down, buddy," the policeman said. "Don't yell at the lady's cat."

"Careful with him," Amy said. "Those burns are superficial, but he might have a concussion."

"Okay, pal, we're gonna take a little ride to the station," the policewoman said.

"Unhand me, at your peril!" Anton bellowed. "That cat is no cat! He is an evil spirit of the nether planes! He is the demon Sholoth-Uul! He will tell you with his own treacherous mouth! He speaks!"

"Fine, we'll get statement from him later," the policeman said, leading Anton to the squad car.

"Speak, Sholoth-Uul!" Anton cried out. "Show these unbelievers your true self! I command you to speak."

By the time the squad car drove off, reds and blues flashing, a small crowd had gathered around the door to Amy's home.

"Um, hi, everyone, sorry for the noise," she said. She jabbed her thumb at the retreating squad car. "Computer dating, am I right?"

Later, after she bolted and locked the door, Amy set to piecing her apartment, and her life, back together. She shuffled through the debris on the floor, gathering up the scattered sheets of her story of witches and black magic and supernatural romance...

Glimpses of her own prose impinged on her mind as she strove to put the sheets back in order. She stopped, regarding the sheaf of papers in her hand. Fluf sat staring at her, lazy left eyelid and all, his tongue protruding slightly.

"Fluf, you wouldn't think anything of mine was vapid, would you?" Fluf gave her a slow blink in lieu of a response.

Amy sighed. "You're a cat, so you probably would, yeah."

Her gaze made several rounds from the cat to the front door to the laptop on the floor.

"Vapid, huh?" she said to herself. "I'll show that puffed up psycho who's vapid."

She threw the papers to the floor, then righted her desk and retrieved the small computer, setting it primly in the dark square it had made in the faded imitation cherrywood. She pulled up a chair, crossed her fingers, and turned the power on. The laptop beeped and started the boot-up sequence, intact save for a small spider-web crack in the upper corner of the screen.

Fluf wandered over to rub against her calves. She scooped him up and placed him on the desk beside the laptop. Inspired, grinning from ear to ear, Amy began to write.

Fluf

by

Amy Barrow

"*Good evening, Miss Baudelaire,*" *said a voice from out of the darkness.*

Anastasia Baudelaire shrieked and jumped, her keys and groceries tumbling to the floor. She whirled and spotted the silhouette of a man sitting in her club chair in the dark. Anastasia darted for the bed across the studio apartment and groped underneath, but found nothing.

"*Oh, no,*" *she whispered to herself. "My French dueling sword is missing!*"

The intruder snapped the antique Tiffany light on. Anastasia turned, her motions effortlessly elegant and naturally graceful. The man matched his voice perfectly: tall, virile, elegantly dressed in a close-fitting Armani suit, with impeccably-groomed brows and a salt-and-pepper goatee and piercing dark eyes.

Amy read back what she'd written and practically squealed with delight.

"Look at that, Fluf," she crowed excitedly. "What d'you think?"

The runt Persian leaned forward, as if to sniff the screen, then turned to look at Amy.

"Get to the part with the cat," he said.

Mimi

KITTEN ANGELS IN NEW ZEALAND:
A WHOLE LOT OF POOP AND A WHOLE LOT OF LOVE
Grace Bridges

TWO OR TEN OR FIFTEEN AT A TIME, ONE HUNDRED AND FIFTY KITTENS have been fostered in my home over a span of several years. All it required was space in my house and lots of room in my heart. My friends told me they would never be able to do it, saying goodbye to the foster kittens as they're adopted. My answer: those kittens are going to new homes so I will have room for more kittens. If I didn't let them go, who would care for the next litter? We are many fosterers. They call us kitten angels.

I encourage anyone to have a go at fostering. There is such great need, and it lets you have kittens on a temporary basis if you're not sure about keeping one for life. The rescue will usually cover the food, litter, and vet costs, so it's a great way to care for cats if finances might be an issue. For me, it was a joy to have kittens in my house at all times, and my friends liked to come over and help with their development, also known as playing with them.

There's no hiding that you deal with so much poop, and kittens make more than adult cats somehow. But there is also so much playtime and snuggle time that scooping the poop is a small price to pay.

I ended up adopting four kittens myself. First, sisters Sunshine and Starlight who were born under a dumpster and retrieved by another volunteer before coming to me at six weeks old, one Christmas Eve. Sunshine, the golden runt of the litter, could sit in the palm of my hand when she arrived, but now is long and strong and one of my constant companions. They are now eight.

My girls have three other littermates and two more foster mates, who were all adopted out to other families in early 2017. I stay in touch with most of them. One brother recently moved to Spain, and I'd say that's pretty good after starting life in the street! The foster mates were given French names and taken to kitten kindergarten by their new parents.

Our rescue group, Gutter Kitties, has a focus on street cats in different ways. One is the Paw Pad, a halfway house for adult cats learning to live with humans — who arrive in three shifts a day to scoop the poop and spend time with the inhabitants. Another branch is the kitten rescue, answering calls about mamas and newborns found outdoors or in people's sheds or garages, and getting them into foster care while they are still young enough to be fully tamed. The younger they are, the easier it goes. The mama cats — often barely mature — can be wary of humans. Sometimes they respond well to kindness and can be adopted out just like their kittens. Others may head off to the Paw Pad once their little ones are weaned. Sometimes, too, I took on adults from the Paw Pad who showed positive development in getting along with humans, to accelerate their progress in a home and help them become adoptable.

Sometimes they scared me, like Moses, the dapper tuxedo who bit me when I tried to pick him up. Another volunteer took him on and managed to tame him where I failed. I am thankful for the wide network of rescuers who are there to help each other in these situations. Moses got a family of his own in the end.

Sometimes they broke my heart, like the little fluffy calico Opal who came in with a bad case of cat flu and couldn't be saved. Her black brother Onyx was adopted together with Sunshine and Starlight's huge ginger brother Gandalf.

And sometimes an adoption wouldn't work out, and a kitten would come back to me after a few days or weeks with a family. Given extra care, they found their people in time.

Vet runs were regular — for desexing and vaccinations, or when the little ones were unwell. Once, a big ginger lad somehow undid his carry-cage door and sauntered across the receptionist's desk to say hello. Over the years I learned lots about giving medication — pills or paste or eye ointment, since many kittens have conjunctivitis when they come in from the street. Flea and worm treatments; baths and grooming; skin treatments for infections; coaxing tiny ones to eat when they come in with no mother; finding my favorite cat litter (it's pine pellets forever for me!). Two older kittens had pneumonia and required antibiotics twice a day for over three months. I ended up adopting Moonbeam and Aurora, now five, and very intelligent although never fully tamed due to having little human contact before twelve weeks of age.

It was also my job to get photos of the kittens and let the coordinator know when they were ready to adopt, while writing introductions for online advertisements. Then I interviewed the applicants. At times it was delicate work to match up the right kittens with their humans. Families with young children needed confident, unafraid pets, while cautious cats were often paired with single folks or young couples.

My housemates over the years have variously tolerated or assisted my efforts, helping to feed and clean up, helping to cuddle and play and tame those who were afraid. Occasionally they would end up being adoptive parents, too.

Many times I wish I could have adopted more of my fosters, like the Maine Coon girls or the litter of five different colors. But after my fifth, Midnight, joined me via the cat distribution system, I have enough on my hands for now.

I have moved to another town where my situation currently doesn't allow for fostering. But one day, when things change again, I can well imagine that I'm not yet done with cat rescuing—because there are *always* going to be more kittens.

MAN'S BEST FRIEND
Nancy Jane Moore

Yeah, I know, I've never been much for cats. Real men don't do cats, that's my motto. But, hell, the poor little bugger was sitting out there in the rain, scratching at the sliding door—you know my apartment's got that patio door, opens onto a little grassy area in back—yowling pitifully and looking wet and bedraggled.

Since Laura left I've developed a little more compassion for those in pain. So what the hey, I let him in and toweled him dry as best I could. Found a can of tuna in the cabinet. Boy, did that make him happy. He scarfed it right down, then settled in to lick himself the rest of the way dry.

Nice-looking cat, once he'd cleaned himself up. Big green eyes, grayish stripes—I think you call it tabby. Not too big, and kind of lean, like he went out and got his exercise going after mice or something. He leapt right up into my lap, made himself at home, and started to purr.

Well, hell, that suckered me right in. I'd been sitting there, planning to take him to the pound. Feeling a little guilty about it—I always figured taking them to the pound was just the civilized version of putting them in a bag and throwing them in the creek. But once he started purring, I got to thinking that maybe having a cat wouldn't be so bad.

So your wife walks out, you get kind of maudlin, okay? Laura had told me I was boring, and I'd started to think maybe I was. I liked it, getting affection from someone. Even a cat. I scratched his ears, and he purred some more. I felt kind of good for the first time in a month or so.

Anyway, I hear pets help you live longer.

Eventually it occurred to me that cats got to eat regular, and they can't just run out to Mickey Ds when they get a mind to. Only I didn't have another can of tuna. Plus he was going to need a bathroom sooner or later, and I did know you can't just send cats outside twice a day to do their business, like you do dogs.

So even though the rain was still coming down, I went out. This big guy was walking just ahead of me in the hall—must have come from the elevators. Really big guy. Beefy. Looked like he might have played linebacker. He let the front door slam back in my face.

His black Firebird was parked next to my old Toyota in the tenant parking area. I'd noticed the car a few weeks earlier—hard to miss the silver racing stripes and mag wheels. He'd probably just moved in. I fumbled with my keys while he screeched tires.

The Giant was full of customers after eleven. I found the pet food aisle and about freaked out. You wouldn't believe how many different kinds of food they got, just for cats. And cat litter—my God, they must have had twenty brands of that, in all sizes.

Fortunately, this woman was loading her cart right next to me. Really loading it, I mean—cans and cans of stuff. Turned out she had three cats. And she wasn't some old lady. Kind of a babe, actually.

But she took pity on me. "Keep it simple, for now," she said. She selected a box of dried food, told me which litter to get, reminded me that I needed some kind of container for the litter, that sort of thing.

"And take him to the vet," she said. "Stray cats can have all kinds of diseases."

I could see this pet keeping might get expensive. I wondered if vets cost as much as doctors.

When I got home I did the usual struggle with the door you do when your hands are full of stuff, finally got it open—and the cat goes rushing out between my legs and up the hall. Kind of surprised me. I guess I was expecting him to be sitting curled up where I'd left him, just waiting for me to come back so he could sit in my lap again.

I put the stuff down and went looking for him. And there he was, up the hall about three apartments, scratching at this door and mewing like his heart was going to break.

So I picked him up, said, "Hey, boy, what's the deal here?" I tried to think who lived in that apartment. You know, life in the big city, you don't really know your neighbors.

After a minute, it came to me. A woman lived there. In her early thirties, maybe. No beauty queen, but not a dog either. Nice enough. Hadn't lived there long. One evening I'd come in the front door while she was struggling with too many bags, and helped her carry them in. And the cat—my new cat—had come running out the door when she'd unlocked it.

Well, what the hell, I could give her all the stuff I'd just bought. I should have thought about asking around to see if anyone had lost a cat. So I knocked on the door. No answer. Knocked louder. Still no answer.

It was after midnight by now, and a weeknight. And it bothered me. Stupid, really, because I didn't know enough about her to know her habits. I mean she seemed quiet enough when we met in the halls, but maybe she liked to party all night. Or was staying with a boyfriend.

But it continued to bother me. I guess it was the cat. I just didn't think she'd go off and leave him out in the rain. So I knocked again. Still no answer.

Well, hell, her apartment would have sliding doors out to the same garden area as mine—that's how the building was designed. So I took the cat back into my apartment—he protested loudly all the way—and slipped out my patio doors. Counted over apartments to figure out which one was hers. It seemed to have a light on inside.

Her sliding door was open just a few inches. I banged on it, yelled, "Hey, lady, I found your cat." No answer. So I tried sliding the door. It didn't move. Must have been jammed open just enough to let the cat in and out, without letting anyone else in.

So I reached my fingers in, and pushed the curtain aside so I could peek in. And saw a leg, lying at a funny angle on the floor.

That's all I saw. It's all I had to see. I went rushing back to my place and called 911.

Well, pretty soon we got cop cars and an ambulance, and even a damn fire truck. Lights flashing everywhere, and all the neighbors outside. The resident manager was standing around, looking a little green. The cops had gotten him to open the door, and he saw her lying there. Blood everywhere.

After awhile they carried her out all zipped in a body bag. And then the cops started asking me questions.

Well, I'd expected that, you know. I mean, I called 'em. But after a few minutes the questions moved from "About what time did you find the cat" to "how long ago did your wife leave" and it finally hit me: they considered me a suspect.

Hell, no wonder nobody wants to get involved. I do my neighborly duty and the next thing you know, I'm going down to the station with a couple of detectives.

Well, they did ask nicely. They didn't arrest me or anything, just said, "Would you mind coming back to the precinct with us?" What was I going to do, say no?

The station they took me to in Wheaton looked like it was built in the seventies—all brick and glass. Some architect probably told them, make it look friendly, not like all those forbidding police stations of the past. Let me tell you, it didn't make me feel any less scared.

First they fingerprinted me— "Just want to check your prints against others on the scene, to eliminate them." Then they asked, would I mind giving them a sample of my blood. Well, of course, I minded. At that point, I thought long and hard about calling my lawyer, only I didn't want to call him in the middle of the night. Anyway he's a divorce lawyer, not a criminal one. So I let them take it. I told them, "Hey, I didn't do anything but find the body. I got nothing to hide."

They stuck me in this interview room and just left me there for awhile. It got kind of eerie, sitting there. I kept thinking I should get up and leave. But maybe they'd locked the door. I didn't want to know that, so I just sat there.

After what seemed like a couple of hours, two detectives came in, and started asking me questions. And you could tell from the questions they really thought I'd done it. The guy was doing this nice-guy routine— "Hey, buddy, I know what's it's like. Your wife leaves, other women shoot you down. You got reason to get angry."

But the woman cop, she jumped all over me. "You hate women, don't you? Your wife said you frightened her, that's why she left, isn't it?"

And I found myself thinking, *My God, did they already call up Laura?* I mean, the scenes between us got kind of ugly there at the end, you know. No telling what she'd say about me.

Then the cop went on about the other women in the building, how they felt scared of me. First I'd heard of it. I had visions of the cops waking up all these women up and down the halls, asking them about the murderer in apartment 107.

They kept it up for about an hour or so and then disappeared for a long time. The room really started to get to me. Nothing to read. No television or anything. Nothing to do but sit there and think. And I didn't have anything to think about, except how scared I felt.

I swore to myself I'd just demand to call my lawyer when they came back. I didn't want to—I figured only guilty people needed lawyers and anyway I'd already paid all my money to lawyers during the divorce—but I began to think I'd never get out of there without help. I remembered some sociology professor I had back in college saying, "It's not whether you're guilty; it's whether you look guilty."

They didn't come back in until about seven o'clock in the morning. And when they did, the male detective started in the on the nice-guy stuff again. Brought me some coffee—kind of old—and a donut from the vending machine. The woman cop just sat there, kind of sullen, watching him get all palsy-walsy with me. And I thought, *well, he's not so bad a guy. I'm not going to need a lawyer here. Truth will out.*

And just as I got comfortable—the caffeine and sugar giving me a pleasant buzz—the woman started in again. She just jumped all over me, mentioning the web sites I'd bookmarked—hell, I mean, my wife left me, okay. I'm not dating anybody. So I checked out some kinky web sites. Cheaper than buying *Hustler*.

I kept looking at the male cop, and he'd give me one of those shrugs, like "sorry, buddy, nothing I can do." And I didn't think it would ever stop, until finally just one thought remained in my head: confess. Just tell them what they want to hear, and they'll leave you alone.

I almost did. You know, we got the death penalty in Maryland these days. Guy kills a woman like that—a sex crime—everybody's going to want to give him one of those lethal injections.

I knew that, and yet I still came that close to confessing. Scary, really, what psychological tricks can do to you. Make you wonder whether you actually did something.

I'm not sure what I would have done if another officer hadn't stuck his head in, pulled both cops out of there. They left me sitting there about ten minutes, long enough to pull myself back together, and realize I'd better demand a lawyer before I confessed to every unsolved murder in twenty states.

And then the male cop came back in, said, "You can go home now. We've got everything we need." Didn't explain a thing. But he did ask a uniformed guy to drive me home. While I was waiting for him, I heard someone mention something about the lab tests coming back. I guess my blood didn't match.

Thank God for modern science.

I saw the woman detective sitting at her desk, just drinking some coffee. She gave me a look as I left. Didn't seem apologetic, just disappointed.

I got back home at maybe ten in the morning, thinking mostly about crawling into bed. I could hear the elevator doors open when I was unlocking my apartment door, but I didn't pay any attention. Frankly, I was leaning up against the door frame, trying not to fall asleep before I got inside. The cat came out, rubbed against my ankles, and then growled. Before I knew it, he ran up the hall, climbed up the leg of this huge guy standing there, and started scratching his face. I swear he was trying for the eyes.

I said, "Oh, shit." It was the new neighbor, the one I'd seen the night before. The big one. He looked even bigger in the morning light. He swatted at the cat, cursing.

Well, I rushed up there, got an opening, grabbed the cat by the scruff of the neck, and pulled him off. Probably took some skin. The guy reached toward the cat, like he wanted to strangle him, which I admit didn't seem like an unreasonable reaction, but I held the cat out of range, and said something dumb like, "Bad cat." The cat hissed at me, wriggled around, scratched at my wrist, which made me drop him. He raced off down the hall to God knows where.

I told the guy, "Man, I'm really sorry about this. Look, let me get something for those cuts." I figured, better be conciliatory with this guy, because both he and I knew he could take me apart with one hand.

Funny thing was, he didn't seem particularly angry. Or not at me, anyway. He rubbed a scratch, looked at his fingers, saw blood, and said, "Damn cat." And then, "Yeah, I guess I'd better clean up."

So he followed me along. I grabbed a couple of towels and the antibiotic cream out of the bathroom. He wiped the blood off, threw a towel on the floor, then started putting the ointment on the cuts he could find.

I said again, "Man, I'm really sorry. I don't know what got into him." After all, I was thinking, if this guy doesn't beat the crap out of me for sure he's going to sue me.

He didn't seem to be listening. He said, "You got any beer?" I pulled a Rolling Rock out of the fridge — I keep it around for my friends who don't know what good beer is. He popped the top and chugged about half of it. And then he said, "That bastard cat never did like me."

I got it, then. He didn't think the cat belonged to me. Which meant he knew who the cat belonged to. Which meant . . .

Freaked me out, I tell you. But I kept my cool. "Just can't tell with cats," I said.

He swigged the rest of the beer, crumpled the can, threw it at the trash. It missed. "Yeah," he said. "Cats and women. You just can't tell." And walked out.

I waited a minute or so, then called the cops. Again.

At first, they acted pretty skeptical. "The cat recognized him?" the male cop kept saying. But they finally agreed to come look at the stuff the guy had touched.

The blood on the towel matched some they'd found it her apartment. Not to mention the nice fingerprints he'd left on the beer can. The cops were sitting in his place waiting for him when he came home.

Turned out he'd killed several other women the same way. He'd move into some big anonymous apartment complex like mine, get friendly with some woman living there—preferably someone new to town, somebody who didn't have many local friends. After running into her a few times in the hall, acting friendly, he'd ask her out. And by that point, he wouldn't seem like a stranger.

He was always careful not to be seen with the women. A couple of months after the murder, he'd just move on to a new place. And start the pattern all over again.

Gives me the creeps, just thinking about a guy like that.

The *Washington Post* did a feature piece on me, all about how sometimes neighbors do get involved in this ugly modern world. Kind of nice, actually. Ran a picture of me with Fred curled up in my lap. That's what I decided to call the cat. Fred. Just seemed right, you know.

Actually, Fred should really get the credit. I wouldn't have found her except for him. And I wouldn't have seen the guy if Fred hadn't attacked him, much less invited him into my place to clean up. They say cats aren't too smart, but Fred knows his enemies. And his friends.

No, I think I'll pass on another beer. Got to get home and feed Fred. I've got a date later. Didn't I tell you? The reporter who did the story. She doesn't think I'm boring.

THE THING ABOUT HUMANS
Christopher J. Burke

THE THING ABOUT HUMANS…" THE OLD GRAY CAT BEGAN HIS STORY, TO the delight of the kittens seated around him. Then he licked the back of his left front paw and rubbed a spot behind his ear.

A little black-and-orange-striped tom jumped up, edging forward. "What's the thing? What's the thing?"

Grizabella had been resting by the fire, just behind the littlest ones. She stepped into the circle, lifted the kitten by the scruff of the neck, and put him back in his place. "Settle down, Rum Tum." She nodded to Old Deuteronomy, then returned to her spot, circled three times, and reclined next to little Skimbleshanks.

Old Deuteronomy rested his chin on his paws and continued his story.

"The thing about humans is that they had three different names. Sounds mad, does it not? But it was true. First was the name that the world would know them by. They had a family name, which was the name of their clan or their pride. Something like Smith or Jones or Black or Green. And they had a given name, which is where it gets funny. You see, the given name is the name the family would call them. And a human cub would be given both these names!"

The kittens rolled around, laughing at this silliness. Victoria bumped into Electra, and the two started wrestling until Grizabella hissed, then they snuggled together instead.

Old Deuteronomy coughed and continued. "The second was their fancy name, like Crazy Joe or Sally-Boy or Brainiac or Nicky Tree Fingers. Names used by their closest friends in the other clans."

The little calico, Plato, lost interest in the tale when she spied a spot of light before her and readied herself to pounce. Old Deuteronomy reached out a paw and smacked Mistoffelees on the back of the head. The all-black kitten yowled, and the conjured light disappeared, to Plato's disappointment.

"However," Old Deuteronomy continued. "They had a third name, a unique name. This was the name that only the human knew. This was the name for how they saw themselves. What they desired. What they strived for. Some of them searched their whole lives to discover what this name was. Some never found out."

Rum Tum sat up on his hind legs and swat at a mote of dust, illuminated by the fire behind him. "They didn't know their own names?"

The old cat shook his head from side to side. "No, little one. Many never discovered their true calling. Imagine a tabby going through the motions of hunting mice but never knowing why they hunted."

Rum Tum's eyes grew wide, and he tilted his head sideways until he almost turned over. "I don't get it."

Old Deuteronomy ruffled the fur on the top Rum Tum's head and smiled. "You will, my boy. One day."

Mistoffelees rolled onto his back, cackling and punching the air. "What a silly story! And you're falling for it!"

"Am not!" Rum Tum shot back. "Besides, it's true. Old Deuteronomy doesn't make up his tales!"

In an instant, the black cat flipped over again, sitting on his haunches. "If it's true, then where are these humans now? What happened to them? Humans are as real as fairies or ogres or elemaphants!"

"They're gone. They left us." Grizabella barely looked up, stroking young Morgan's matted fur. "They had their day in the sun, and they moved on."

Old Deuteronomy rose and circled little Mistoffelees, who spun around, not wanting the old cat to get behind him. "Some say they went up into the sky to find a new world. Some say they went down into the dirt and were no more. But up or down, they once were here." He sat back and searched the night sky. "Wherever they are, if they still are, they've gone from this place. It's ours now."

An ember popped in the fire, sending up a geyser of sparks. The little cats jumped and ran to watch the show, chasing down every twinkle and flicker. Storytime was forgotten.

Old Deuteronomy padded his way beside Grizabella. "Ours now," she repeated, nuzzling under the older cat's chin. "And it will be theirs when, like the humans, we're just memories."

"The Thing About Humans" was previously published in In A Flash 2020, eSpec Books, 2020.

THE MOST UNLIKELY OF PLACES
Danielle Ackley-McPhail

Living in the city—or even just the boroughs—you see a lot of unexpected things, but the tiniest of kittens—a grey and white tabby—jumping out of a pile of tires to pounce on a guy working on a jacked-up taxi was not one I was prepared for. My imagination saw too clearly what could happen to that tiny cat in that scenario.

Forget about the fact I was waiting for the bus that would begin my two-and-a-half-hour compute to work; and forget about the fact that my mother-in-law had made her stance on bringing any more cats into our shoebox apartment quite clear. I got out of the line waiting for the bus and scooped up that little tabby, pretty much the size of my two palms together, and beelined for our apartment across the street.

As I came through the door, the first words out of my mouth were "I know! I'm just grabbing a carrier!" my plan being to stop at a vet office I knew of on the way to work and surrender the kitten. I popped her into the bathroom for holding and went to dig out the carrier. When I came out (less than a minute later) both my husband and my mother-in-law were already enthralled by her, but said nothing as I put her into the carrier and went off to my interrupted commute.

Well… best laid plans, and all that, right?

After a bus ride, a trip on the subway, and a walk-through downtown Manhattan, I arrive at the vet office only to be told they couldn't even find homes for the kittens they already had. I hadn't yet told them why I was there, so I quickly redirected to asking them if they could tell me what the sex of the kitten was, said thank you after they confirmed I had a girl cat on my hands, and then went to work.

Fortunate for me I worked for a small family-owned publisher and I was allowed to keep the kitten with me as I worked. Now… trying to keep her contained was another matter. She leapt out of any box I put her in only to climb onto my desk and up my arm to curl up on my chest. By the end of the day we had bonded, and the publisher decreed that from then on I was in charge of any cat books.

Oh… and as I returned home still hauling the cat, walking into the door with my plan B—surrendering her to our own vet—already coming out of my mouth, my mother-in-law firmly announced that by no means was I surrendering her cat.

She was promptly branded "Goodyear" (tires, you know.) and we later discovered that she was, in fact, a fully grown cat! Goodie never did get any bigger, and she held our hearts for the rest of her (many, many) days.

Goodyear's take-your-kitten-to-work gotcha day.

SMART SPACE CATS
Anton Kukal

THE OTHER CATS PACED, SLEPT, OR GROOMED THEMSELVES, BUT I JUST SAT and watched. We were confined to cages, stacked in tall columns from floor to ceiling against the wall. Thick metal wire stood between us and freedom. This was the animal detention facility on Muninn Station, orbiting the second moon of planet Heimdall, in the Balder System of the New Eden Galaxy. Captured and caged, our futures were known. They were short. They were bleak.

A battered metal desk stood at the room's center, cluttered with the tools of our capture: snares, bait boxes, adhesion plates, tangled netting, and the netgun that had captured me because I had been too clever for the traps. The officer's chair behind the desk sagged with split plastic seat covers, its cushions hemorrhaging yellow foam. Recycled air whispered from the ceiling vent, carrying the scent of engine grease, synthetic cheese, and old musk.

The sliding door grated open with a grinding sound.

Officer Gabe entered the room. He was a slouch of a man in a grey jumpsuit smudged with old stains. His breath smelled. His body reeked. He had been fired from almost every job on the station before landing this one. Unfortunately for the cats of Muninn, he enjoyed cruelty and had a talent for stalking.

A woman entered behind Gabe. She was tall, lean, and wore the flight suit of a nomad mercantile trader with the name Nyelle stitched above the right breast pocket. Her expression unreadable, she studied the cages. A man followed her into the room, also wearing a nomad flight suit. His nametag read, "Tarn." He was holding hands with a young girl whose pocket did not bear her name. I sniffed. The child had the mingled scents of both. She was their offspring.

"Take any you like." Gabe, the animal control officer, said. "We got plenty. Grab two, if you want. Or three."

Nyelle scanned the cages, her voice level. "We're looking for just one pet."

"They're all beautiful," the girl exclaimed, running over to the cages.

"Be careful, Silo," Nyelle warned, hurrying to stand behind her daughter.

She peered into the cages while her mother hovered protectively.

Across the room, standing with Gabe, the father murmured. "I've heard things. People say these station cats are smart."

Gabe shrugged.

Tarn pressed his question. "They can open cabinets. Unscrew lids. Lost Earth cats can't do that."

"They're still cats. Fur clogs the air filters. They piss in the ducts, spreading their musk."

"But they're smart?" Tarn pressed.

"They came from Amon." Gabe admitted. "Station admin purchased them as part of a plan to control the rat population. Worked stellar. Now, stray cats are the problem. They got into the food units. Started breeding. Not many rats left, but the cats are everywhere."

The man frowned. "We don't want a terraformed abomination."

"No abominations here," Gabe said quickly. "House Arvellon spared no expense terraforming Amon. These cats all tested within Lost Earth norms. They just seem a bit smarter."

I snickered. If they only knew how smart we were. I and the other Amon cats could understand their language and read their letters. We could open doors and easily circumvent their traps. I didn't understand their numbers. I knew one was one, but more was many. We were smart in the ways that counted. Even Lost Earth felines weren't dumb, not by the standards of dumb in the universe. Now dogs… dogs were dumb.

"We don't want a thinking cat," Tarn whispered. "Do you have a Lost Earth one?"

The officer shrugged. "I can't tell the different cats apart."

"Nyelle," Tarn called. "These cats aren't for us. We'll look at the next station."

"You said that at the last station," the girl said, her voice trembling.

"Dear," the woman said with a bit of exasperation. "We've been to three different facilities. The rescues are all the same. We promised Silo a pet. You cannot keep putting this off."

Tarn waved his mate to his side. "These Amon cats can open doors and avoid traps. People say they are smart."

Nyelle chuckled. "How smart can a cat be?"

"This isn't funny," Tarn said. "I don't want my daughter exposed to a bioengineered predator."

"You're just finding reasons," Nyelle chided.

Silo wasn't paying attention to her parents' discussion. She was kneeling at a bottom-row cage containing a white-and-brown kitten with her fingers pushed through the metal wire. The cat was just a little larger than me, but it wasn't an Amon breed, and it couldn't think in human speak. Its thought projections were just instinctual desire and base emotions.

The station officer jabbed a thumb at our cages. "Makes no difference to me. Take one or not but decide by tonight because the captain signed the order this morning. We're spacing 'em all tomorrow."

My ears twitched. Spaced. Tomorrow. I knew it was coming soon. When the cages were filled, the cats were brought to the airlock, and with the inner door sealed, the outer door was opened to the vacuum of space. Death was coming to us all, but maybe one of us might escape. Maybe it might be me.

The Lost Earth cat wanted out of the cage. He was pushing his desires into the girl's mind. She was responding. They were both building their relationship at a subconscious level. Lost Earth cats were limited to influencing with base instinct, but the augmented cats of Amon could project words into their emanating thoughts. Speaking the human language seemed to give me greater access to their subconscious awareness, which created stronger connections.

I sent my thoughts out. Silo noticed me as if I'd made a mental noise that attracted her attention. I watched the girl come to my cage. I wasn't compelling her. Cat communication doesn't work like that. Cats exude our desires and emotions. We can comfort. We can request. These subconscious emanations help form the cat-human bond. I've seen the same in dogs, but dogs are stupid and lazy. Other animals have it too. Humans call it domestication, but it's always a mutual pairing.

Silo couldn't have been more than seven years old in the way humans measure time. Thin face. Hair like the color of electric wires with the insulation chewed off. Coppery and shiny, braided with silver beads that clinked softly. Her eyes were dark like her mother, but her slim nose had come from her father.

"Pick me," I thought, shaping the words as all Amon cats could. I pushed the desire gently into her mind, weaving my emotion with the word-meaning. Around me, the other Amon cats were doing the same. Each of us was desperate to be saved. The cats of Lost Earth lineage just wanted to get out their cages to roam free in the station, but the Amon cats could understand the coming danger. We did not want to be spaced.

Silo smiled at me. I knew I was reaching her. The other cats didn't have a chance. I was the smartest feline in the room. My mental projections were the strongest.

"Mama," she whispered. "I want this one. Look. He's all black."

The woman examined me carefully. Her older mind was harder to reach. Harder to influence, but I tried. "Me. Take me."

After a moment, she sighed. It was half-resignation, half-amusement.

"Alright," she said. "But you're cleaning the litter tray, understood?"

The officer opened the cage, and I walked into the girl's arms. She pressed her cheek to my flank. Her father scowled. I sent him warm thoughts, calm and welcoming, but he subconsciously blocked me. His dislike of all things furry was a wall against my influence. Many humans were like that. They had no love for their furry friends, and so they spent empty lives without the companionship of a pet.

The woman thanked the officer, and we left the room. The other cats called after me, wishing me luck. They bore no ill will. We Amon cats never fought against each other. The emanations faded as the door slid shut. I suddenly felt very alone. A cat's range of influence was not very far.

"One puddle," Tarn said. "And that cat goes out the airlock."

Silo gasped and hugged me tightly to her chest.

"Your father's joking, dear," Nyelle said, giving Tarn a look that made it clear he better be joking.

I did not sense he was joking, but the child trusted her mother, and I vowed to only urinate where the humans wanted me to. I'd even use their toilet, if it made the father happy.

We had almost reached the docking bay when the explosion came. A roar of noise followed by a wash of heat. I could hear people screaming and running for the ends of the passageway, perhaps trying to reach the vertical shafts that tied into the core of the station.

The corridor shook as secondary explosions occurred. Smoke surged. Lights flickered and went out. On both sides of the hallway in which we stood, massive sealing doors slammed down as the decompression alarm wailed. The whole structure lurched throwing us all against the wall. The girl cushioned me, and the father cushioned the girl.

Gravity failed, and we floated together in the center of the corridor, spinning, until the humans' magnetic boots clicked on and stuck them to the wall. Tarn pulled everyone to the floor, not that it mattered if we walked on the walls or ceiling. I could feel the corridor tumbling through space. Was it no longer attached to the station?

"Silo?" Nyelle whispered, her voice thin.

"I'm okay, Mom."

Emergency lights came on, bathing the hall in red. Wires dangled from the ceiling. Panels hung loose. Debris floated everywhere. The four of us were alone in the dim hall. The family and me.

The father pulled a port from his hip pocket and consulted the screen. "Terrorist attack. The Free Planet League is claiming responsibility."

The mother moved to the porthole in the bulkhead. She gasped as she looked out into space. "The bomb blast broke us free. We're drifting away."

I wiggled from Silo's grasp and floated to the viewing pane. The stars spun wildly. Dizzily. The station flashed into view. The blast had exploded one of the vertical shafts to which our ring corridor had been attached. Without the column's support, the centrifugal force of the spinning station had broken us free and tossed our fragment into space. Unchecked, the momentum was carrying the corridor further away. Every time the station appeared, the structure looked smaller.

Silo came up behind me, and I let the girl take me into her arms. She nuzzled my flank, and I pushed a calmness that I did not feel into her. She sighed with contentment. Human children readily responded to cat thought. Adults, not so much. I could not help Tarn and Nyelle with their anxiety.

The mother pulled an emergency oxygen canister from the wall. "One canister. For the three of us. Three hours of air. That's it."

"The rest of the ring?" the father asked, looking to the doors which had slammed down.

Nyelle checked the door controls. "Only this corridor has survival pressure. The others are at twenty percent or less. Anyone there is likely dead."

Tarn nodded grimly.

"We'll share the bottle," Nyelle announced, her voice steady, as she handed the breathing mask to Silo. The girl moved to put the mask over my muzzle.

Tarn shook his head. "The cat doesn't get any."

"Shadow is part of our family," the child protested.

"We need all the air." The father shook his port. "Station rescue is busy at the station. We need to last as long as possible."

"How long?" Nyelle asked, looking at the single cannister.

"Nevermind," Tarn said softly. "Let the cat have a pull. He's part of the family."

Silo placed the breathing mask over my muzzle, and I drew in the sweet cool oxygen. She held it there for a moment. Then took some for herself before passing the bottle to her mother and father. The cycle began.

"The rescuers are too busy at the station," Tarn whispered. "They won't come in time."

I understood why the father relented. He didn't want me to die in his daughter's arms. He wanted me to die after his daughter passed out. Being smaller, I would be the last to die. He would let me be a comfort to his child for as long as possible. I sent out calming thoughts to them all. Love and kindness and peace.

"That's space," Nyelle said resignedly. "Life and death in the black."

The family huddled together against the bulkhead, magnetic boots holding them to the floor despite the lack of gravity. The tank soon sputtered, and realization settled into the young girl.

"When are they coming to save us?" she asked.

"Soon," Tarn promised. "Let's all try to take a nap."

"We need more oxygen," Silo said.

Her parents did not respond.

"There's oxygen in the adjacent sections," Silo said hopefully.

Tarn shook his head. "We cannot open the doors."

"The atmosphere is too thin," Nyelle explained. "The lack of pressure will kill us."

The red lights blinking along the ceiling of the corridor were starting to dim. Power would fail soon. The air was already getting colder. There, in the middle of the ceiling, was a small vent. The electrostatic pressure screen prevented atmosphere from leaving the room, but it would not prevent the passage of a solid object. Like me. I knew the ducts in the ceiling would carry over to the adjacent corridors. Opening the doors would depressurize the whole corridor. With no way to re-pressurize, we would all die, but in the adjacent corridor I could survive the lower pressure for a few moments, long enough to reach the tank and get back to safe pressure.

I pushed off from the girl. The momentum carried me up to the vent, and I slipped through the screen. The duct stank of scorched metal and old cat musk. My paws pushed me through the chill metal tunnel. The pressure here was a little less than in the room, but not enough to hurt me. It was actually good as the lower pressure would help my body to adapt slightly.

I reached the ceiling vent of the next compartment. Two bodies floated in the space. A maintenance worker in her station uniform and a miner with a dirt-smudged face, likely fresh up from the planet for some rest and recreation.

Pushing through the membrane, I felt the pain of low pressure. I opened my mouth to let the air in my lungs equalize. My head throbbed. My chest burned. I still tried to breathe. There were trace amounts of oxygen in the atmosphere, and any little bit would help. Floating down to the cabinet, I opened the door and pulled the tank loose with a paw. I would not have been able to move the tank in normal gravity, but in zero g, it floated easily. Clenching the strap in my teeth, I dragged it behind me like a tail. I reached the vent and took a deep breath. I pulled the tank through. It barely fit.

Returning, I dropped the oxygen canister next to the mother's hand. Her eyes widened.

"The cat is trying to save us," Nyelle whispered.

I turned. No time to rest. The oxygen in the corridor was being used up, and one new canister was not enough for a family of four. Back into the duct. The opposite way this time. I hurried through the tunnel to the other adjacent corridor. Six bodies floated there. Five children with a single adult. A school class on an outing? The teacher had opened the cabinet to get the oxygen tank for the children but did not have time to remove the canister before the pressure dropped. Her sleeve had caught on the latch, and she floated there tethered by the cloth.

I descended to the cabinet and nosed the canister loose. It floated. I bit the fabric strap and pulled. I was beginning to feel the lack of air now. My pulse throbbed in my ears. Loud, like drums. My thoughts were slipping toward instinct. Back through in the duct, I had to take a moment to recover. The cumulative effects of rapid transitions from pressure to no pressure had hurt my body. I dragged the canister more slowly, but I made it back, dropping the tank beside the father's feet, as if to prove my usefulness.

"Six hours to live." Tarn cursed me softly. "But rescue still won't come. We're only three people and too far out. There are too many on the station still needing to be saved."

Nyelle leaned against him. "Six more hours together is a blessing, my love."

He held them both. I curled beside Silo. I had done my best to help them and to save myself.

Sleep came for them one by one. The father first. Then, the mother. Then, the child. Her grip on my body slackened. I was losing consciousness when an impact shook the corridor. A moment later, sparks sprayed down from the ceiling. A thick metal square of bulkhead floated inward, its edges still red hot from the cutting torch. A rush of air flooded into the corridor. I revived almost instantly with just a few deep breaths.

A man in a black flight suit emerged through the smoke swirling around the hole. He carried three emergency oxygen tanks. His name tag read, "Vincent." The patch on his left sleeve identified his ship as the ShatteredSun.

He scanned us using a hand-held med-scanner, his face hard, all businesslike. "Three alive."

He knelt beside Silo and placed the mask gently on her face.

"You came for us?" Tarn whispered accepting the offered mask. "You said you couldn't."

"We're not station rescue," Vincent replied. "We're independent operators."

I knew the words independent operator was another way to say mercenary. These were not humanitarians. They were profiteers. They would charge for the rescue, and if the family could not pay, they would leverage the debt against their ship.

"We heard the GalNet chatter and jumped from Helios," Vincent explained. "We vectored to your estimated position. Like finding a pearl in the ocean."

"Jumped?" Tarn looked like he would have preferred suffocation over rescue by profiteers. He was about to lose everything. Galactic Law gave the rescuer the right to repayment for all rescue expenses and profiteers always padded those bills.

A woman pushed down into the corridor. She had long auburn hair that framed an oval face. Her silvery jumpsuit shimmered in the red emergency lights.

"You should have just let us die." Tarn sighed.

"Don't be silly," the woman said lightly. The name on her jumpsuit read, "Rebecca."

Tarn clenched his fist. "I can't afford jump fees! The fuel costs…"

Rebecca offered a wide, friendly smile. "Are none of your concern."

"But…"

"We're not indenturing you." The woman waved away his concern. "We're rescuing you."

"Without charge?" Nyelle asked, incredulous.

"We fly the frontier," Vincent said. "Out there, it's not like the Prime System. On the frontier, people are still neighborly. People help one another."

Tarn shook his head in disbelief. "Galactic Law gives you the right to…"

"To ruin you?" Vincent asked. "To take your ship. To indenture you… or worse, leave you to beg employment station-side."

Tarn nodded.

"Not my style."

"Thank you." Tarn started to cry. So did Nyelle.

"Let's get you on board the ShatteredSun." Vincent said.

Silo carried me in her arms as the family floated up to the ceiling and entered the mercenary's ship. Rebecca took us to the medical bay as Vincent went forward to the cockpit. The ShatteredSun detached from the drifting corridor with a loud metal clank and then vibrated as the vector engines engaged.

Rebecca spent the next few minutes checking Tarn, Nyelle, and Silo. and then announced. "You're all fine." She passed the medi-scanner over me and added, "Even the cat."

Moments later, the engines shut down, and the ship jarred ever so slightly as the Muninn Station docking clamps pulled the ShatteredSun into position. The airlocks aligned with a dull thudding sound.

Vincent met us at the airlock. "Off you go."

"Thank you so much," Nyelle said.

"Happy to help. Just pay it forward, if you can."

"We will," Tarn promised.

Vincent reached down and scratched my head. I allowed it.

Silo looked up to meet the mercenary's eyes. "Shadow saved us."

"Saved you?" Vincent asked.

"He got the oxygen canisters from the other locations."

"The cat did that?" Rebecca asked.

"This one did," Silo said. "He's from Amon. They're smart cats."

"Interesting," Rebecca said, exchanging glances with the pilot.

"If you want one, they got more on the station," Silo said, putting a protective hand around me.

"We're not star traders." Vincent smiled. "But a trading ship might find smart cats to be a valuable commodity."

The two mercenaries returned to their ship.

Silo followed her parents from the docking bay, carrying me tight against her chest. Tarn turned right at the first intersection.

"Our ship is that way," Nyelle said.

"Yes," Tarn acknowledged. "But that merc had a point. Let's go rescue some smart space cats."

Hootch

ABOUT THE AUTHORS

Marc L Abbott is a Brooklyn native horror author. He is the co-author of *Hell at Brooklyn Tea* and the two-time African American Literary Award-winning horror anthology, *Hell at the Way Station*. His horror short stories are featured in the anthologies *Blackened Roots, A Woman Unbecoming, Soul Scream, Even in the Grave,* and the Bram Stoker Nominated horror anthologies *New York State of Fright & Under Twin Suns: Alternate Histories of the Yellow Sign.* His new horror novel, *Sinister Ascension* from Mocha Memoirs Press, is out now. He is a 2015 Moth Story Slam and Grand Slam Storyteller winner and an award-winning actor. When he is not curating workshops for the Center for Fiction, he teaches writing to students at Dr. Izquierdo Health and Science Charter School. Find out more about him at www.whoismarclabbott.com

Award-winning author, editor, and publisher **Danielle Ackley-McPhail** has worked both sides of the publishing industry for longer than she cares to admit. In 2014 she joined forces with Mike McPhail and Greg Schauer to form eSpec Books (www.especbooks.com).

Her published works include eight novels, ten solo collections, three writers' guides, and two cookbooks. She is a former member of the Science Fiction and Fantasy Writers Association and a current member of the Horror Writers Association.

Danielle lives in New Jersey with husband and fellow writer, Mike McPhail and four extremely spoiled rescue cats.

Rigel Ailur writes in almost every genre, but mostly science fiction and fantasy. Her short story credits include "Brigadoon" in the *Star Trek* anthology *Strange New Worlds 10,* "Building Bridges" in the IAMTW's *Turning the Tied,* and "Class Project" in *Double Trouble: An Anthology of Two-Fisted Team-Ups. The Angel Cat Collection* includes two stories by her, and the *Lady Pirates* omnibus *Pirates!* includes four of her stories, two about the Queen of the pirates in the Asian seas, and two about Medieval English river pirates. Her novel *Azure Dragon* takes place in contemporary America, and the many novels and short stories of her *Tales of Mimion* series, including one auf Deutsch, take place on that planet. Above all, she treasures her most beloved swarm of cats. Visit http: BluetrixBooks.com for more information and a complete bibliography.

Charles Barouchhas five stories on the Moon. He also has stories available on Earth at hdwp.com. He's been published in SF/F/H, humor, Western, and more, by CEP, Canyons of the Damned, Dusty Saddle, Shebat Legion, Fantastic Books, and others. His podcast: hor-rorwords.com. Join him on bluesky @hdwp.com

James W. Bates is a writer, content creator and creative consultant who has contributed close to two-hundred stories on over forty intel-lectual properties. He began writing professionally almost immediately after graduating from film school at Ithaca College. He has written for numerous television series and comics such as; *LEGO: Star Wars, Trans-formers, Timon and Pumbaa, The Penguins of Madagascar* and *Simpsons Comics*. James was the Head Writer for three seasons of the *Power Rangers* franchise and during that span it was the most watched Kids' Action Show in the world. In 2022, Bates wrote and co-produced the short film *The Invitation*, which has been screened in festivals on four continents. Early in his career he also served as a creative executive at Walt Disney TV Animation and a Director of Development at the Fox Kids Network.

Originally from southern New Jersey, James now lives in Califor-nia with artist and writer Karen McDaniels Bates. They share their home with three spoiled cats and their yard with a revolving cast of well-fed feral kitties.

Grace Bridges is a fantasy and sci-fi author, a professional fiction editor, and is currently responsible for five cats. She lives in New Zealand's magical geothermal heart amongst geysers and hot springs, and often sets her stories there. Previously she has fostered cats and kittens for Gutter Kitties, an Auckland-based rescue group. A three-time winner of the Sir Julius Vogel Award from the Science Fiction and Fantasy Association of New Zealand, she also belongs to the Rotorua Arts Village Collective and is a life member of writers' association Speculative Fiction New Zealand (SpecFicNZ) after serving as its president for seven years. www.gracebridges.kiwi.

Christopher J. Burke is a math teacher, a webcomic creator, and writer from Brooklyn, where he does a lot of walking. He cowrote GURPS *Autoduel* for Steve Jackson Games, and his work has appeared in in *Daily Science Fiction, MetaStellar, Science Fiction Lampoon, Free Flash Fiction, MAD Magazine,* and the anthology *Devilish & Divine* (eSpec Books). His books include *In A Flash 2020* and *A Bucket Full of Moonlight* from eSpec Books. He's self-published five short fantasy books in a series called Burke's Lore Briefs, the latest of which is *Yesterday's Villains*.

Artist **Amber Davis** currently fosters for the South Jersey Regional Animal Shelter, in Vineland, NJ.

Jacob Jones-Goldstein, founding member of Oddity Prodigy Productions, is an internationally published author, journalist, and editor. His short stories have appeared in anthologies and magazines such as 'Plague of Shadows' from Smart Rhino Press, 'Beach Pulp' from Cat & Mouse Press, and Lovecraftiana from Rogue Planet Press. He has two novels, 'The Change' from Oddity Prodigy Productions, and 'The Last Summer', from the Systema Paradoxa series of Espec Books

He has edited the volumes 'Scary Stuff', 'Beneath the Yellow Lights', 'Bright Mirror', and 'Where Legends Walk' also for Oddity Prodigy Productions.

In addition to fiction, Jacob writes about music for his personal site, ShoutingStreet.com, and has covered the Philadelphia 76ers for several online publications. Beyond writing and editing, he hosts the popular podcast "The Scary Stuff Podcast", plays Magic the Gathering, Disc Golf, and way too many board games.

He loves comic books, movies, exploring, cats, family, friends, Joel Embiid, Tyrese Maxey, and his wife, Jennie.

Eric Hardenbrook is a fan, an author, and an artist, usually in that order. He lives in central Pennsylvania where he writes to try to get the stories out of his head. When he's being a fan he helps runWatch The Skies and assists in the publication of their monthly fanzine. He can be found (at least some of the time) at The Pretend Blog. When not working on those things, Eric enjoys board games and is an old-school role player, running Groves of Inan on YouTube.

Brad Jurn is an office furniture manufacturer who moonlights as a sci-fi author. His love for science fiction began at the age of four when his parents took him to see *Star Wars*. He became a Star Trek fan at age fourteen, and has been in love with the franchise ever since. Brad's writing career began in 2019 when he wrote a masked hero story titled *The Brick*. Since then he has become a yearly contributor to the *Brave New Girl's* anthology series. This series features teenaged girls who excel at STEM in a sci-fi setting. In 2024 Brad wrote a Star Trek story titled *The Three-Legged Dog* which was featured in the web magazine *Engage*. Brad is currently writing a pulp adventure tale titled *Curse of the Inca's Tomb: A Rollins and Harrison Adventure*.

Kris Katzen's novels include the alien thriller *Curai'Nal*, the intergalactic adventure *A Little Piece of Home*, and the rollicking outer space chase *Escapes*. Her short stories appear in the long-running *Brave New Girls* anthology series and *Bad Ass Moms*. *The Angel Cat Collection* includes two stories by her, and the *Lady Pirates* omnibus *Pirates!* includes two of her stories about interstellar pirates who use magic. Her story "Kaboom, Ka-bye" led off the Shadowrun sourcebook *Seattle 2072*. Most importantly, Kris dotes on her astronomically adorable feline kids. Visit http: BluetrixBooks.com for more information and a complete bibliography.

Anton Kukal is an author, actor, and adventurer. After serving in the United States Army as an armor officer, he graduated from law school and enjoyed a highly successful legal practice, then he decided to embrace his creativity. Anton is now a full-time writer. His fiction appears in the award-winning *Defending the Future* anthology series. His website is antonkukal.com.

For nearly 50 years, until his death in 2024, **Sharon Lee** and Steve Miller lived, wrote, and kept cats together. Working on the theory that you can't have enough of a good thing, they brought cats in to comfort and confound the large cast of characters inhabiting the Liaden Universe®, their long-running space opera. Likewise, Sharon made sure cats were represented in her single-authored fantasy trilogy and cozy mystery duology. "Ginger and the Bully of Lowergate Court," which appears in this volume, is unique in Lee and Miller cat tales because it actually happened. Yes, exactly the way I said.

Will McDermott turned a love of science fiction and games into a writing career. He has published nine novels, more than twenty short stories, and helped create innumerous worlds, characters, and stories for card, board, and video games. His fiction is often set in gaming universes, including *Magic: The Gathering, Warhammer 40K, Renegade Legion Universe*, and *Mage Wars*. He is known for bringing larger-than-life characters alive, including Warhammer's Kal Jerico and Mad D'onne, Magic's Balthor the Stout and, more recently, Night Stalker's Carl Kolchak. Check out willmcdermott.com, w_mcdermott on Instagram or willmcdermott.author on Facebook.

F. R. Michaels is just a nice, normal person who happens to like weird and scary stories. Seriously. An IT guru, retired church elder, and garage-band musician, his true love is writing about the strange little people who live in his head. His work has appeared in Alfred Hitchcock's Mystery Magazine and Haunts (as Frank Michaels) as well as the anthologies *Strangely Funny II, Mysterion, Wicked Weird, Wicked Creatures, Monstorm, SVP's Little Black Book of Terror*, and *The Chaos Clock*. He dwells on Long Island and writes horror and dark fantasy.

Nancy Jane Moore is the author of the fantasy novel *For the Good of the Realm*, the science fiction novel *The Weave*, and the novella *Changeling*, all from Aqueduct Press. Her short fiction has appeared in a number of anthologies and magazines and in her collection from PS Publishing, *Conscientious Inconsistencies*. A native Anglo Texan, she lived in Washington, DC, for many years and now lives with her sweetheart in Oakland, California. She has lived with a variety of cats, many of whom just showed up one day. Currently she is working on a sequel to *For the Good of the Realm*.

Lisanne Norman began writing when she was eight because she couldn't find enough of the books she liked to read. In 1980 she moved to Norfolk, England, a year after joining The Vikings!, the largest British re-enactment society in Britain. There she ran her own specialist archery display team. Personal experience has always provided inspiration for her writing, and the more of the world she traveled and experienced, the richer she found her life and the reservoir of creativity for her writing.

Now living in California, she has an anthology of Fantasy stories out called *The Pharaoh's Cat* published by eSpec Books. She also has the Sholan Alliance series published by DAW.

in that series, she has created worlds where Warriors, magic, and science all coexist. As well as these books, she has many Science Fiction, Fantasy, and Historical short fiction stories published in DAW anthologies, as well as with eSpec Books in their Defending the Future series.

There's been a debate among certain obscure and drunken literary scholars about whether **Patrick Thomas** was raised by Cthulhu or a leprechaun in a Manhattan bar. What there is no arguing about is that Patrick is the award-winning author of 50+ books including the beloved fantasy humor Murphy's Lore series, the darkly hilarious Dear Cthulhu advice empire, as well as the Bikini Jones books, the Mystic Investigators series, and the creator of the *Agents of the Abyss.* His other books include the Hexcraft and the Terrorbelle series, *Exile & Entrance, Cryptid Fight Club*, and the mystery *Assassins' Ball* co-written with John L. French.

Dear Cthulhu has expanded from magazines and books to broadcast monthly on the radio show Destinies: The Voice of Science Fiction. Over 100 of his stories have been published in magazines and anthologies. A number of his books were part of the props department of the CSI television show and Nightcaps was even thrown at a suspect's head. His urban fantasy *Fairy With A Gun* at one point had been optioned for film and TV by Laurence Fishburne's Cinema Gypsy Productions. Top Men Productions has turned his Soul For Hire Story, Act of Contrition, into a short film.

As Patrick T. Fibbs, he writes middle readers including the Babe B. Bear Mysteries, The Undead Kid Diaries, Joy Reaper Checks Out, the YA Emotional Support Nightmare, and the Ughabooz books for younger kids.

Visit him at www.patthomas.net and www.patricktfibbs.com.

Sherri Cook Woosley holds a master's degree in English Literature with a focus on comparative mythology from the University of Maryland. She's a SFWA member, and her short fiction has been published in *Mmeory, Abyss & Apex Magazine*, and *Dreamforge Magazine*. Her speculative mystery novelette *Mother's Instinct* was released by eSpec Books in fall 2024. Additionally, Sherri's first children's book, *Postcards from a City of Monsters,* is based on her Pushcart-nominated short story "Gargoyles in Prague." The children's book was published by Improbable Press in August 2024 and won a Mom's Choice Gold Award in 2025. Find her on Instagram @Sherri.Woosley or at www.tasteofsherri.com.

Jeff Young is a bookseller first and a writer second – although he wouldn't mind a reversal of fortune.

He is an award-winning author who has contributed to the anthologies: *Afterpunk, In an Iron Cage: The Magic of Steampunk, Clockwork Chaos, Gaslight and Grimm, Phantasmical Contraptions and other Errors, By Any Means, Best Laid Plans, Dogs of War, Man and Machine, If We Had Known, Fantastic Futures 13, The Society for the Preservation of C.J. Henderson, Eccentric Orbits 2 & 3, Writers of the Future V.26, TV Gods and TV Gods: Summer Programming.* Jeff's own fiction is collected in *Spirit Seeker, Written in Light* and TOI *Special Edition 2 – Diversiforms.* He has also edited the *Drunken Comic Book Monkey* line, *TV Gods* and *TV Gods –Summer Programming* and is the managing editor for the magazine, *Mendie the Post-Apocalyptic Flower Scout.* He has led the Watch the Skies SF&F Discussion Group of Camp Hill and Harrisburg for twenty-two years. Jeff is also the proprietor of Helm Haven, the online Etsy and Ebay shops, costuming resources for Renaissance and Steampunk.

Spot and Spec - The Initial Interview

HOW CAN YOU HELP?
GLAD YOU ASKED!

Not up to cat rescue field work?
There are still plenty of ways you can help.

Volunteer at your local shelter.

Foster, if you are able.

Donate rags or blankets.

Look up your local shelter or rescue's online Wish List and
donate something they need.

If you see an animal in distress, call your local rescue, or at
least the police non-emergency line.

Pick up volume one, *A Future for Ferals*, to learn more about
cat rescue and also help us help them!

Tell people about these charity anthologies
so we can do more to help the cause.

All profits from *A Future for Ferals* and *More Futures for Ferals*
will be donated to cat rescue organizations and shelters.

OUR COOL CATS COLONY

Alexander Hale
Alp Beck
Amanda Sedivy
Amelia B.
Andreja and Duke
Andrew Hatchell
Andrew Kaplan
Anna Marie Stern
April Sue Billings
Aunty Meow
Beth Lobdell
Bethany Jezerey
Brad Ackerman
Brendan Lonehawk
Brooks Moses
Bunrab
Caroline Westra
Carrilyn Thorpe
Catherine Asaro
Cathy Green
Cheryl Lynn Chessie Jones
Christopher J. Burke
Colleen Feeney
Connor Lehmann
Craig Hackl
Danielle Ackley-McPhail
David Lee Summers and Kumie Wise
DC
Deborah A. Flores
Dev Singer
Dianne Nicholson

Dr. Karen
Ed Ellis
Ef Deal
Elyse M Grasso
Florentina
George Minor (Aspen & Daisy)
GhostCat
Gillian Daniels
Gina DeSimone
Giusy Rippa
Glori Medina
Harriet McDermott
Holly
Ivy Ru
Ixias
Jacob Jones-Goldstein
Janice and T Campbell
Jeffrey Harlan
Jeremy Audet
Jeremy Bottroff
Jerrie the filkferengi
Joanne B Burrows
Jonathan H. Bruck
Joshua McGinnis
Juanita J Nesbitt
Judy A Lauer
Judy McClain
Katy Manck
Kay Hafner
Kris smelser
Leanna Renee Hieber
Lee Hawkridge

Linda Pierce
Lisa Kruse
Lorraine J. Anderson
Louise & Ruby McCulloch
Lynn P
maileguy
Margaret Bumby
Margot Harris
Marie Devey
Mark Woodson
Mary Anne Howard
mdtommyd
Melynda Marchi
Michael Gordon
Michael S. Rosenberg
Mike McPhail,
    McP Digital Graphics
Nellie Batz
Norman Jaffe
Paksenarrion
Peter Piine Graham
pjk
Reckless Pantalones
Richard Novak
Robert H Hudson Jr

Ronald H. Miller
Ruth Ann Orlansky
Sabrina White
Samantha J Bryant
Sarolta
Shawnee M
Sheryl R. Hayes
SilverWolf28
Sonya Lawson
Stacey Helton
Stephanie Wood Franklin
Stephen W. Chappell
Steven Purcell
Taj S.
Tanya Koenig
The Initiative Inn
The Watanabe Clowder
Tina M Noe Good
Tory Shade
Tracy Popey
Tracy 'Rayhne' Fretwell
Trip Space-Parasite
W. Scott Meeks
Walter J. Montie
Zilla

Daisy, backyard Colony Cat